| | | |
|---|---|---|
| AUTHOR'S NOTE | | 3 |
| OPENING POEM: | A Snail's Point of View | 4 |
| FOREWORD | | 5 |
| CHAPTER ONE: | The Night in Question | 7 |
| CHAPTER TWO: | A Loaf of Bread | 12 |
| CHAPTER THREE: | The Executioner's Axe | 16 |
| CHAPTER FOUR: | Daggers | 20 |
| CHAPTER FIVE: | The King's Brother | 25 |
| CHAPTER SIX: | The Night of Questions | 28 |
| CHAPTER SEVEN: | The Golden Arrow | 33 |
| CHAPTER EIGHT: | The Knight and the Priestess | 39 |
| CHAPTER NINE: | Thick as Thieves | 48 |
| CHAPTER TEN: | The Night is Long, Part One | 60 |
| INTERMISSION | | 67 |
| CHAPTER ELEVEN: | The Night is Long, Part Two | 70 |
| CHAPTER TWELVE: | The Gaudy Crown | 74 |
| CHAPTER THIRTEEN: | Robin Hood | 84 |
| CHAPTER FOURTEEN: | Matching Coats | 92 |
| CHAPTER FIFTEEN: | The Golden Sword | 98 |
| CHAPTER SIXTEEN: | Rest and Respite | 104 |
| CHAPTER SEVENTEEN: | A Trial by Chess | 112 |
| CHAPTER EIGHTEEN: | The Storm, Part One | 122 |
| CHAPTER NINETEEN: | The Storm, Part Two | 127 |
| CHAPTER TWENTY: | The Storm, Part Three | 134 |
| INTERMISSION TWO | | 142 |
| CHAPTER TWENTY-ONE: | A Viable Plan | 143 |
| CHAPTER TWENTY-TWO: | The Day in Question | 152 |
| CHAPTER TWENTY-THREE: | Trials | 158 |
| CHAPTER TWENTY-FOUR: | The Fall | 166 |
| CHAPTER TWENTY-FIVE: | Robins in the Day | 177 |
| EPILOGUE ONE: | The Corridor | 179 |
| EPILOGUE TWO: | The Backwards Pack | 181 |
| EPILOGUE THREE: | The Painted Mermaid | 184 |
| EPILOGUE FOUR: | Pond Weed | 186 |
| EPILOGUE FIVE: | Poems about Dresses | 187 |
| AFTERWORD | | 194 |

Dedicated to my mum, Sarah. Thank you for giving me life, food, a roof and Wi-Fi.

Without you this book wouldn't exist, for many reasons.

## Author's Note

This book has twenty-five chapters, an author's note, an opening poem, a foreword, two intermissions, five epilogues and an afterword.

The first intermission is pretty explicit.

So if you're not into that sort of thing, or you're reading this in a church and would rather not be seen partaking in what can only be described as sins of the typeface, maybe skip the intermission.

Other than that, you should be fine, unless you don't like books, in which case you've made a bad decision.

- *Dajo*

## ~A Snail's Point of View~

What is that, over there, in the distance?
Could it be something worth seeing?
I shall try to get to it.
It is very far away, or it is very small, or both.
But I am also very small, and also very far away, if you think of it the other way.
How much have I moved?
Very little.
Very, very little.
My trail is small…
And it is light, now.
Where is the darkness?
Where is the rain that dripped on me?
Where, in fact, am I?
What is this new texture underneath me?
What is the shadow?
Is it the darkness?
It is moving very quickly.

# Foreword

Legends speak of a man named Robin Hood.

They talk of his valiant deeds, of his courageous feats, of his noble exploits. They talk of how this man, this single man, stole from the rich and gave to the poor. They speak of his merry men, and of his bow and arrow, and his green tunic. They speak of him in hushed, reverent tones. They speak of him in loud, exuberant chants. They speak of him in story books.

The legends are, as is to be expected, fundamentally wrong.

Deep in Shorebark Forest, up a stone path that winds around brambles and ponds, through a rusted gate and down a treacherously unstable rocky slope is a tavern. Tonight, a full moon rises amongst rainclouds. The sky is ready to rain, and the moon watches, waiting for the downpour. An old woman steps outside. She is not tall, her face is covered in enough lines that one with enough talent could write music between them, and her eyes glow a brilliant blue under the white light of the sky which pierces through layers of leaves.

She is closely followed by another woman- this one tall, strong, and stoic. She says nothing. The older of the two says much. She talks of the old days, of the times when she was young, and of times yet to come.

They stand together, for a while, before drops of soft rain begin to finally make their descent after hours of preparation, waking snails and sending the weary to sleep. They step back inside, and the moon watches on.

Inside is warmer, away from the gaze of the moon and all else who might be staring. Ale flows freely, and food is shared happily when not being thrown.

There are boots of all styles and sizes warming by the fire, and jackets hung by the door. In the corner, a young man plays the lute, and from across the room another man watches, enraptured.

The old woman and her companion walk behind the bar and enter a back room. This room has no windows, only a round table and seven chairs. They sit, and the old woman talks more while the other woman is silent more.

A third woman enters, younger than the first two. She gives an update, and the two women at the table nod, satisfied. The third woman leaves, temporarily.

This is The Golden Arrow, and it is home to all who have nothing. It is the home of the poor that the rich have taken from. It is the home of happiness in a world where good humour is hard to find.

The legends say that this is where you can find Robin Hood, if you care to look.

But of course, the legends are fundamentally wrong.

## Chapter One: The Night in Question

Shovel in, dirt out, pile it up next to the gravestone, repeat as necessary. Simple enough. With enough practice it shouldn't take very long at all. Open an old grave, take any valuables, leave, and sell the valuables as quickly as possible. Easy.

Marian Stoke had done this a hundred times. She had it down to a precise art, in and out before the taverns close and down to the docks in the morning. She was the master of avoiding detection. She checked her pocket watch, laced up her boots and pulled up her cowl, heading out and treading lightly on the cobbled path down to the cemetery. To the untrained eye she was invisible under the oak canopy bordering the road and she was entirely certain there were no trained eyes watching her.

She'd visited a lot of graveyards in her time. She found the best ones to be the unguarded ones- ones where the groundskeepers weren't paid enough to care, and ones where the coffins weren't nailed too tightly. The graveyard here in Knottwood represented a perfect storm, in those regards.

An old man who smelled strongly of cheap beer stumbled out of a tavern that smelled strongly of old men. Marian froze, waiting, anticipating his next move. If there was one thing she'd learned about how to predict drunk old men, it was that you can't predict drunk old men. Everything about this man was a shambles. In motion, he resembled an injured horse. Even standing still, he swayed like a pendulum. His ancient, unwashed coat ruffled slightly in a gust of wind that shook the leaves above Marian's head, breaking the silence with a rustling white noise. Then, the silence broke again, as the man moved across the road. To say he walked would be inaccurate, he seemed to just fall forward and allow the whims of the night to carry him safely. It was almost graceful, like an intoxicated swan, which Marian would later learn was in fact the name of the tavern the man was expelled from.

He got closer, close enough for Marian to smell his breath. Surprisingly, it didn't smell too terrible. It was just the rest of him that smelled of alcohol and regret. He hadn't noticed her yet. She had feared he would catch a glimpse of her in the light that spilled from behind him when he tumbled out of the bar but evidently his senses were too impaired to notice even a hand slipping into his pocket and confiscating his watch. For a moment she thought perhaps this man was so far removed from reality that she could steal his hat. This thought didn't linger in her mind for long, it would be senseless and far too risky to steal the hat from his head. She knew she definitely should not try.

After stealing the hat from his head, she continued down the path.

She'd walked this road many times before. Not that you'd be able to tell. If she ever left a trace, it'd be washed away soon enough by the rain that plagued the city and the many trampling feet that walked the streets in the day. In the ambiguous light of the sun lazily pushing through thick layers of cloud, the city was as busy as a city can possibly be. The citizens were aware of the weather not fulfilling its half of the deal of existence so they put extra time and money into never sitting still, determined to never let themselves blend in with the background. That wasn't the life for Marian though. The background was where she felt comfortable. Not from any anxiety or shyness- rather from a simple desire to reach her ends by any means necessary. She took what she wanted and what she wanted was usually money.

It wasn't a long walk to the graveyard, and each step was ingrained in her mind, her legs working on muscle memory, her stride confident and deliberate but effortlessly quiet. She reached it without further incident. The drunk man from earlier most likely had to be up early in the morning. Earlier than everybody else, that is, in this city of early risers. The gates were tall and locked, totally impossible to get past at this hour, but the walls were short and open. Marian swung over the wall, bare hands on brick, and landed softly on grass, barely breaking her stride. Her heart was as still as the night, beating in hushed tones. Her breath was calculated and controlled. There was a shovel she kept hidden behind the tallest tree. She found the grave she'd marked the previous night and got to work. Just like every other night, Marian was in her element, piling dirt next to a headstone. She knew there was going to be something brilliant in this one, the grave of a stuffy old banker. It had been here, dormant, for years, every night the same, until tonight. This was the night this grave was robbed.

Shovel in, dirt out, pile it up next to the-

"You're getting dirt on my shoes."

Stood in front of Marian was Priestess Trinna.

This was wrong. This was all wrong. This was the most wrong possible. There was not supposed to be anyone here- in all Marian's time grave robbing, this was the first time she had been caught. She was frozen in terror. The wind nipped at her uncovered fingers.

"Take off your cowl." Trinna demanded, folding her arms. Marian slowly, carefully, obliged.

They looked at each other in dim light. Marian couldn't hold eye contact. She felt shamed- like a child found stealing biscuits. Trinna moved closer.

"You have come into my graveyard- this sacred place, this RESTING place, and the only resting you have done is- is this HAT. Is this YOUR hat resting on the headstone? Judging by what you're doing here I assume you stole the hat too. Give me a good reason why I shouldn't report you at once. Two counts of robbery- a grave and a hat." Trinna exploded, ranting in anger.

Their breath formed clouds in the cold air. A couple of drops of rain fell every so often. The pause went on for almost a full minute while Marian tried to think of an answer, or a solution, or an escape route, and while Trinna folded her arms even tighter, refusing to budge.

"You're Marian," said Trinna, suddenly calmly, "You're Marian from the college. Is this what you do all the time? Are you... Are you the one that does this?"

Marian looked up, realising she had been staring at her feet for quite some time. She finally met Trinna's eyes.

"Yes." Marian replied.

Trinna inhaled, then sighed. She unfolded her arms, and looked down at the grave.

"Put it back. If you've taken anything, just put it back. Cover the grave, take this, this hat- which is a man's hat, you definitely stole this- and go. Just go, Marian."

Marian was once more stunned into silence.

"You want me to go?" she asked, shyly, fearing a trick or a deception. She wondered if Trinna planned to attack her. She thought she could probably take Trinna. Trinna was broad-shouldered, tall, and muscular for a priestess, but Marian had speed on her side- speed and a shovel, if it came to it. A shovel which she tightened her grip on now.

"Yes. Go. You're... Forgiven, this time, as long as you don't come back." Trinna sighed, waving her hand as if to shoo Marian away.

Hesitantly, Marian moved the dirt piled next to the grave back into the hole she'd left. Trinna stood and watched until it was done, and then spoke once more.

"Why graves, Marian? Can't the dead just be dead? You're a talented girl, Marian, and I wish you wouldn't do this, but if you've got this kleptomaniac itch to scratch, why not do something good with it? I don't know- take from the rich, give to the poor, that sort of thing. Instead of just for personal gain."

Marian bowed her head in silence. She wasn't sure what Trinna was saying.

"Anyway. Go. Please, go. The rain is coming again- you don't want to be inside now."

And Marian left. She walked away from the graveyard, and back onto the cobblestone road, and back to her house, where she proceeded to fall backwards against the inside of the front door and slowly collapse onto the carpet, crying quietly. She had been caught. That just wasn't supposed to happen. Guilt began to wash over her as rain washed over the town.

Back on the cobble path, a drunk man stumbled home. Wind tickled the tips of his ears- where was his hat? He thought he must have left it in the tavern. Never mind. It didn't matter now. Hats are rarely of consequence to men who are losing their heads in the morning. He rooted around his pockets for his house key- noting to himself that he must have left his watch in the tavern too- and, finally, poured himself through the door into his house.

It wasn't a very nice house, especially compared to the ones closer to the square in the centre of town, and along the road between the forest and the docks. The halls were narrow and awkward, the walls were bare and boring, and the carpet had maybe once seen better days but had long since lost all recollection of them. But it was a functional house. There were stands for coats and for hats, there was a kitchen, there was a bed, there was a second bed which was never used, and there was a chair. It was all he needed.

He motioned to put his hat on the stand, having momentarily forgotten it was missing. He sighed and collapsed into his chair, and there was silence. It wasn't a very nice silence. It was filled with thoughts of what would come afterward. It was filled with thoughts of tomorrow.

He unfurled a crumpled letter he had been keeping in his pocket. Below a royal stamp, the letter began formally:

"By the order of the King's Stead, Sir Patton Cross is to be executed on the Fifth of the month.

Mr. Cross stands accused of thievery, treason, resisting arrest and drunken behaviour. He has stood before a court of judges who have decided upon his death. If Mr. Cross fails to attend his execution date, his next of kin will be brought to Knottwood Tower and justice will be dealt.

Kind Regards,

Leonard Garden-Hand, steward to the King's Stead and Chief of the Guard"

Patton sighed and dropped the letter, holding his head in his hand, beginning to drift to sleep. It wasn't a very nice sleep.

Unbeknownst to all, a fourth figure stood under the trees outside Marian's house, hidden in darkness and behind the fuzz of the rain. They watched through a window as Marian stood, brushed herself down, and left the house again.

## Chapter Two: A Loaf of Bread

Sir Patton Cross lived alone. He had lived alone for most of his life. He would live alone for the rest of his life. His house was humble, functional, and as he sat, stewing, contemplating tomorrow, he wondered if in the next life, he would have a more comfortable place to rest.

His chair was brown, for the most part. The cushion was grey. There were a couple of tears on the arms and the back right leg was slightly shorter than the others, and so had to be held up with an old book titled "Pond Weed: What's it all About?". Patton had no intention of ever reading it, because although he knew that one should never judge a book by its cover, he was relatively certain that any book with the name "Pond Weed" wasn't worth his limited time. The chair was in front of the fireplace, which was rarely ever lit.

Lighting the fireplace was too much effort these days. It was infinitely easier for Patton to just wrap himself in a blanket than to go out and chop wood just to burn it for a few hours of heat. The blanket was rough, and was so old, and so tired, that it almost needed its own blanket. It had been stained by years of neglect, and had absolutely seen better days. But it did the job it was there for. It kept Patton warm on cold nights, and dry when the ceiling leaked during heavy rain.

Heavy rain fell down on Patton's decrepit house, leaking through the ceiling. A wayward drop stumbled squarely onto his forehead, waking him from light sleep. He was sweating, and for a moment wondered why before realising he'd forgotten to take off his coat when he came in. He didn't know how long he'd been sleeping, but he felt a little more sober than earlier, and it was still extremely dark. It wasn't the time for his execution yet.

His execution order had said "thievery, treason, resisting arrest and drunken behaviour". He didn't know why he was being *executed* for that, though in all honesty, he suspected his punishment would have been less severe if he had not had the audacity to have been born black.

He thought back to the events of the night in question.

He had been walking along the docks, trying to find a fisherman's stall still open after sunset, and after a while of walking, there one was.

He looked over the fish for a few moments, and made idle chatter with the stall owner. They talked of the weather, of the catches of the day, and they made a brief mention of Patton's time as a knight of the King's Guard, though that had little to do with the price of fish.

Before Patton could buy a meagre morsel, the stall owner was called away by a town guard. These guards were separate from the King's Guard- town guards simply patrolled the streets to maintain the law, whereas the King's Guard were warriors who generally fought overseas, spreading the King's influence by expanding his empire.

At the moment, the King was away, visiting one of his many cities. In his place, sat on the throne at the capital city, was his younger brother, who ruled infinitely more harshly than the King ever had. The guards at the docks now were there on the orders of the King's brother, seeking out the perpetrator of a series of recent thefts. Apparently three shops had been broken into in the past week. As the guards questioned the stall owner on anything suspicious he'd seen, Patton turned back to the stall.

At the back, behind the stall's actual products, was a loaf of bread. A loaf of bread would fill Patton up for tonight and for most of tomorrow. A loaf of bread would be perfect.

But with the guards right there, Patton thought twice. He couldn't possibly take the loaf of bread. They were there investigating crimes- how would it look if he stole something right in front of them?

But then, he thought perhaps he could outrun them.

But what if he couldn't?

But it was bread.

But what if they caught him?

It was bread. He needed the bread. He needed food. He took the bread.

He'd thought about it for too long. A guard turned and saw him slip the bread under his coat, and caught up to him when he tried to run. They took him in for questioning, in the tower, and they interrogated him about recent thefts and other crimes, and he rightfully, correctly, denied all knowledge. He wasn't a criminal, he was an opportunistic starving veteran, but they didn't see it that way. To deny the charges, to be uncooperative, was treason under the new laws set in place by the King's brother. He had had one drink at the tavern earlier that day, and his breath still smelled of ale.

Thievery, resisting arrest, treason and drunken behaviour. If Patton had learned one thing now, it was never to steal a loaf of bread. This thought occurred to him as the Chief of the Guard wrote his execution order, forced it into his hands and shoved him out of the door onto the cobble road he had limped down a thousand times before. His execution date had been set for three days from now.

Now, one night before the event, Patton struggled to fall back asleep. Water continued to drip through the rickety ceiling of Patton's shack through the night, a constant, sluggish drum beat against hard floors and, often, his forehead.

Marian was out again, in the rain. She'd been thinking. She wouldn't let being caught get her down. She saw no point in moping, she didn't see what it could possibly achieve. Happiness was a state of mind, she told herself, and one she was determined to stay in.

She would do something good. Something that wasn't for personal gain, tonight. There were plenty of nights left in her life for her to steal somebody's watch or coin or hat, but for one night she would do as Priestess Trinna told her.

She would take from the rich, and give to the poor.

Striding doggedly through the downpour, she found her way to the tower a street over from the town square. It loomed over the city, twice as tall as any house, a constant imposing reminder to never go against the laws of the land. It was made of a dark grey stone, almost but not quite black, and had a single window near the top- commonly understood to be a bedroom reserved for visiting nobles. But that's not where Marian was visiting, though her intentions were noble for the moment. She would walk around the tower, to the yard behind. She knew precisely what to look for and where it would be.

Finally under the cover of the roofed hut behind the tower, she opened a box. It was bland- decoration was pointless considering the contents.

She took her spoil to the graveyard and hid it near her shovel, noting the unilluminated windows in Priestess Trinna's house.

That night, she took a weapon from the rich and gave life to the poor.

That night, Marian stole the executioner's axe.

## Chapter Three: The Executioner's Axe

The next morning was a busy one, especially by Knottwood's standards.

The butcher on Matthew Street closed up his shop after only two hours of hurried business. The baker down by the docks didn't even open. The café on Rodney Street was full to bursting with people seeking warm drinks. Everybody wanted to watch the execution, and nobody wanted to be late.

The crowd began to form in the town square. The stage had been erected earlier that morning, a sturdy oak structure with a stone chopping block in the centre. Almost the entire population of Knottwood had come to watch the show.

Priestess Trinna woke up, and began her well-rehearsed morning. Tea with no sugar in her old blue cup with a chip in the handle, a slice of neatly buttered bread, dressed and out of the house by nine. She lived behind the church, in a surprisingly roomy bungalow where she kept a beautifully arranged garden. Her house was bordered on all sides by a maroon fence, and the gate opened onto a path up a manageable hillock to the back door of the church. The graveyard was on the right. She didn't want to look at it but her eyes found themselves inexorably drawn in that direction, sweeping over the graves, looking for any sign of what had happened the night before.

She continued into the church, locking the back door behind her, and picked up the Holy Book. It was one of only two copies in the city, the only other being in the library. She didn't like the copy in the library. It was too modern, there were too many pictures and not enough stories.

"It's supposed to be scripture," she had said to the curator of the library on her last visit, "Not a children's plaything. I'm all for them reading, but this? This is an affront to all that is holy."

She rarely visited the library any more. She barely even left this particular corner of the town. Church Road was a straight cobblestone road from the edge of the city down to the docks, and everything Trinna could need was within a five minute walking distance. Every Saturday after a sermon she would walk down to the docks and speak to the merchants, buying fish and other sundries, and trying to convince them that a life at sea was fundamentally unholy. She had little cause to go anywhere else except for parish visits- which happened rarely, as most people just came to the church to see her instead.

She certainly had no cause to visit the town square, which she found overwhelming on a good day. There were always children running around in the fountain when they really ought to be in school, and adults rushing around buying and selling things when they really ought to be in church. Today was even worse, and she wished she did not have to go there.

It was a ten minute walk to the centre of town, though Trinna was not certain how much of that time could be attributed to her own nerves instead of the distance. People greeted her in the street as they pushed past her on the way to watch the theatrics of the day. It seemed to be an exciting day for them.

Having finally arrived, Priestess Trinna pushed her way to the stage through the hum of the audience, climbing up and approaching the chopping block. A lump formed in her throat and she shivered with dread, but she clutched her holy text nonetheless. She looked out over the heads of everybody watching, waiting for the executioner to arrive.

Marian was stood in the crowd. She stared Trinna dead in the eye and took a bite of an apple, nodding solemnly.

She had known Marian since she was a child. She came to her Sunday school every other week, and now she was here to watch an execution, and after the events of last night... Priestess Trinna thought she should probably convince Marian to confess a few sins in the coming weeks. The noise of the crowd mixed with the cascading water from the fountain, which was in turn mirrored by the sweat pouring down Trinna's hands and her forehead. There were too many familiar faces in the crowd- how could they stand to watch this? How could they *choose* to watch this?

Just as dizziness started to settle in Trinna's head, the stomping of heavy boots came from behind her. She turned to see the headsman approach.

He was seven feet tall, and built sturdier than the stage he walked on. His beard covered his neck and his arms bulged with muscle that was almost painful to look at as it stretched the fabric of his shirt. The entire crowd fell silent out of a mixture of fear and quiet excitement.

The sound of bugles came from one of the buildings bordering the square as the king's guard announced the coming of the criminal. Sir Patton Cross was lead out, up onto the stage, and pushed onto the chopping block. More bugles sounded. The headsman gave a thunderous click of his gargantuan fingers to summon his apprentice, who was to bring the axe to end Patton's life.

There was silence. The apprentice did not appear. The headsman clicked his fingers again. The apprentice continued to not appear. The headsman grunted and clicked a third time.

At last, the apprentice broke his trend of non-apparition. The axe, however, remained in a state of absence. Panting and sweating, the apprentice stumbled up the stairs onto the stage, tripped over to the headsman and whispered something to him. The headsman grunted in anger and whispered back. This went on for some time before the headsman grumbled and pushed the apprentice to the front of the stage. The apprentice, little more than a boy, stood in front of the crowd and slowly gained the courage to speak.

"The axe," he shouted with a crack in his voice, "Has been stolen. The execution… The execution cannot continue until it is found."

The crowd roared in anger and disappointment. Patton bolted up in shock, standing and staggering backwards. Priestess Trinna took his hand in solidarity. Trinna, at least, was pleased about this. She hadn't been looking forward to giving Patton's last rites, or the blessings after the event, or the funeral. Naturally, Patton hadn't been looking forward to any of it either, but his heart was beating too quickly for happiness. He had expected to die today.

All the faces of the crowd snarled in complaint, except one. Under the cover of confusion, and satisfied Trinna had seen her and as such would not suspect any involvement- after all how can somebody watching the execution have possibly stolen the axe?- she fled.

On the cobblestone road between the edge of town and the docks, Marian stepped quickly back to her house, an axe in her hands. She began to run as she heard the storm of the crowd, and broke into a sprint when she heard the voice of the headsman strike like lightning as he screamed over the collective voice of the audience to shut them up.

Slamming the door behind her, she threw the axe down into the front room and hastily shoved it under the couch. She'd get rid of it later. For now she just had to keep it hidden. She couldn't believe what she'd done. The whole city- possibly the whole country- would be talking about this for months. She fell back onto the couch, the axe out of sight and hopefully soon out of mind, and wiped sweat from her brow.

Then, she saw her. A woman. In the far corner of the room, leaning against the wall, hands in her pockets.

"For a master criminal, you've got a terribly bad habit of being caught."

Marian's heart began to pound all over again.

## Chapter Four: Daggers

Twice in as many days, Marian had been caught. She was getting rather sick of it. She'd never had this problem before- she'd had no problems at all, really. It had just come naturally to her.

She had two brothers and three sisters, though she had not seen them in years. Last she heard, they had all joined professions people would call honourable. Two were doctors, one was a teacher and- from what Marian could remember- the other two had started their own business selling insurance. But Marian walked a different path entirely from an early age.

Her first memory of stealing was at a market on a family holiday. She remembered adults towering over her, all talking about the most boring things in the world. She remembered thinking about slipping away from them all and going on a little adventure- and that's exactly what she did.

Slowly pulling her hand away from the loose grip of her mother's, she snuck behind stalls and looked around. None of the shopkeepers noticed her as she took money and trinkets- first from the shelves, then from their pockets as she got more daring. She began to realise why they couldn't see her- they didn't want to see her. They were busy, they were only interested in paying customers, they were focused entirely on what was in front of them and didn't care about anything happening behind them.

Eventually, she found her mother again. She was quibbling with a store owner about the price of a vase, saying it was far too much and trying to haggle down the price, though the store owner would not budge. Marian decided to have a little bit more fun.

She walked casually around the back of the stall, dodging the tall legs of adults nimbly and almost effortlessly, slunk under a shelf, and took a whole purse of coins. She then came back out as quickly as she entered, leaving not a single trace of her presence, just in time for her mother to become frustrated and leave.

That day, Marian entered the market with a backpack containing two apples. She left with a backpack containing four apples, forty-two coins, three necklaces, and a diamond ring that was far too big for her juvenile fingers.

She carried on this way for years, and never got caught until that night in the graveyard. And now she'd been caught again. It was, in a word, frustrating.

"Just a joke. I'm sorry- I didn't introduce myself, did I?" the woman in front of Marian continued, "My name's Jemima. It's lovely to meet you, I've been quite a fan!"

Jemima was light eyed, and light haired, and light skinned. Much lighter skinned than Marian. Jemima's hair was also entirely straight, unlike Marian's tight natural curls which refused to be tamed by anything but rain, and she spoke in an accent Marian couldn't quite identify- it was somewhere in England, that much was certain, but it was vague and not at all able to be placed. Marian looked at her, silent, slowly reaching for her pocket.

"I was watching you at the graveyard last night. Harris Trent-Beacon... That's quite the daring grave to go for. Do you know how much they buried him with?"

Marian's hand slipped into the pocket of her jacket. Her grip tightened. Jemima smiled.

"Because I don't know exactly how much it is, but it is just... Lots. I mean, it's *got* to be lots! You know who he was, of course. The chancellor at the bank up until, how long was it now- seven years ago? And they buried him with the entire contents of his personal bank account, which I always thought must have been a bit of an insult to his children, not getting any inherit..."

Marian interrupted Jemima's soliloquy by pulling a small knife out of her pocket and swinging it at Jemima's face. Jemima dodged backwards, then ducked underneath a second swing. Marian stepped forward, pulled Jemima up to face her, and held the knife to her throat.

"You can't just come into my fucking house and start a monologue. You can't. You just can't do that. That's not what people do, nobody ever even visits me, so this begs the question- *Who* are you and *what* are you doing here?" Marian interrogated, her eyes wide but her eyebrows furrowed. For a moment, the room was silent save for their mutually panicked breaths.

"*That's two questions.*" Jemima whispered.

Marian's stare intensified, her eyebrows like an active volcano.

"I'm sorry... This has been a bit rude of me, hasn't it?" Jemima said between breaths, smiling and glancing down at either the knife or Marian's lips, "Look at that. You're not going to hurt me, are you?"

There was another silence, and Marian spoke again.

"I won't hurt you if you just tell me who you are."

Jemima laughed, and suddenly pushed Marian back. Marian tripped and fell onto the couch. She immediately leapt back up again, and swiped the dagger aimlessly in the air, more to scare than to actually threaten. Jemima pulled a similar dagger from her inside pocket with one arm and grabbed Marian's wrist with the other, but Marian resisted and pulled her wrist away, making another empty swipe. Jemima blocked Marian's dagger with her own and with a swift flick, loosened Marian's grip which was already insecure from the sweat saturating her palms, and finally sent Marian's dagger spinning to the floor.

Jemima once again pushed Marian onto the couch, and this time climbed atop her, in a locked straddling position, her arms and legs blocking Marian's escape. They were face to face again.

"Look, I didn't come here to fight you. I'm sorry it had to come to this. I came here because you've attracted our attention."

"Our?" Marian panted, exhausted from a long day already though it had barely begun, "Who's the plural?"

Jemima cocked her head and smirked.

"You know I've never heard it put that way, "the plural", I like it, you've got a way with words- but that's not the point. Last night, you robbed a grave, and you were caught, correct? That was you, I've got the right house?"

Marian's heart was beating quicker than a hailstorm. She barely whispered out a yes.

"Sorry you got caught. My fault. I needed to see how you'd cope under pressure. For what it's worth, you've done well."

Silence reigned in the kingdom of the room but didn't reach the thoughts racing through the republic of Marian's mind.

"We've heard about you, Marian. It is Marian, yes? Either way, we've seen your work at the shops near the docks- very, very good work. Nobody suspects a thing, we've looked at the list of suspects and there's not a single mention of a Marian. And then the graves! The graves are a stroke of genius! To take things from people who lack the ability to miss them is... Wow. I mean I've been at this for years and I'm not at your level. None of us..."

"WILL YOU STOP SPEAKING IN AMBIGUOUS FUCKING PLURALS," Marian burst, "AND TELL ME WHAT YOU MEANT BY SAYING IT WAS YOUR FAULT I GOT CAUGHT?"

Jemima looked wounded, as though she wasn't quite expecting anger. She slowly stood up, away from Marian, rubbed her forearm anxiously and blushed lightly.

"I'm sorry, I thought... Okay. Full story. I'm from... The Hooded Council. We meet every night after sunset in the woods, and... And we steal things. And we saw you stealing things, and we thought you were good, and... Listen, I was wondering if you wanted to... Come for a drink?" Jemima said, nervous hope in her eyes.

"Are you asking me out on a *date?*" Jemima stood, speaking sharply and incredulously.

"I- I'm asking if you want to join... I'm asking if you want to come and steal things with me. With us."

Marian thought for a moment.

"So what you're saying is- you intentionally tipped off the Priestess to somebody being in the graveyard, so I would get caught and you could see how

I'd react. Then- then you watched me take the axe, and knew I'd come back here because you watched me come home, and you waited here to ask me to come to the woods and steal things with you?"

"Yes." Jemima replied, honestly, looking straight at Marian's eyes now but still blushing.

"Then yes." said Marian.

The amount of silences that had filled this single room already today was becoming overwhelming. If somebody had experienced this many silences while stood giving a speech, they would be completely disheartened, but in this room, the silence only served to heighten the senses of the two women in their impromptu staring contest.

"Yes? After...?"

"Don't tell me you expected me to say no when you came in here."

"I mean I had hoped you'd say yes..."

"Come back later. I've got things to do, people to see, and axes to hide. Come back tonight and tell me the whole situation. We'll have both calmed down by then. But the answer's... The answer's yes."

Jemima hesitantly edged towards the door, afraid Marian would attack her either verbally or physically. Sensing no threat, she walked out, and Marian followed her to the front door.

"I'm..." Jemima began, but Marian interrupted.

"Explain later, please."

Marian opened the front door, and gave Jemima a light smile, which was returned, awkwardly. The door closed behind Jemima, who stood in the stark light of day, baffled but relieved.

## Chapter Five: The King's Brother

In the tower of Knottwood, frantic footsteps echoed around the walls of the stairwell. Silence was preferred in these halls out of respect for visiting nobles- generally, tones were hushed, speech being little more than a murmured breath. The walls were solid, the only window being high at the top, accessible only via this circular stairway.

Usually, these corridors carried an air of mystery and worship, but as the Royal Messenger reached the top, running through, panting and gasping as he went, the aura of reverence dissipated as if diluted too rapidly.

This tower was known all over the country- perhaps even the world. It had been built several hundred years ago by the subjects of an ancient monarch who to this day remained nameless in history books, their entire life lost to time. It was decorated with pictures of the ocean depicted as a world far from the touch of humanity, in a numinous bubble between seconds. The lower levels of the tower were presided over by members of the city's court, who dedicated their lives to study and science, only venturing out occasionally to appear at a trial or to visit the library. But today, the peace was disrupted.

The Royal Messenger arrived at the wooden doors leading into the visitor's room, and hastily entered. Sat in front of him, facing the window, was the King's brother, watching a rowdy crowd dissipate below. On either side of the room were servants, and all eyes fixed upon the messenger as he cleared his throat, the King's brother turning, standing, addressing the Messenger directly. His pointed ginger beard vibrating with deep baritone, he spoke and the room almost shook.

"What the fuck do you want?"

"Important news, my lord," the Messenger replied, his voice pitiful in comparison, "Very, very important news."

The Prince, not overly tall but taller than the Messenger nonetheless, waved his hand and gave a grumbling from his chest, urging the Messenger to carry on so that he may return to his day.

"Your lordship... The news is dire and requires immediate action."

The servants, solemn with silk suits and the collective silence of an overly elongated funeral, shifted in worry. The King's brother stared down his nose, waiting, growing impatient.

"My lord... The executioner's axe has been stolen."

The Prince turned with a deep inhale to his seat, looking past it, through the window that looked over the entire town. He saw the crowd had mostly vanished by now, though the executioner still stood with the Priestess on either side of Patton Cross.

His voice deeper and infinitely vaster than the oceanic abyss portrayed on the walls, the King's brother spoke with enough scorn to bring a fertile world to dust. The witnesses of his fury never forgot his words of regal wisdom as they resounded in their minds.

"You have got to be taking the *piss*."

"I, no, sir, I'm not," the Messenger stammered, "Somebody must have taken it from the yard overnight, my lord, and the execution couldn't go ahead..."

The King's brother sighed.

"Come stand at this window. Stand here and tell me what you can see."

The Messenger instantly did what he was told, scared of the consequences of even the slightest indecision. But before he could speak, to tell the Prince what he could see, he was interrupted.

"Here, boy, you can see the town square. You can see the fountain, and the stage erected in front of it. You can see people stood on the stage, and all of them have their heads."

The King's brother grabbed the Messenger's shoulder and gripped tightly. Some of the servants flinched, memories of feeling the same hands.

"Tell me my name, boy."

"Prince William Alan Anchor," the Messenger answered instantly in the voice of somebody who has had a lifetime of rehearsal, "Protector of the Nine Courts of the Anglo-Irish Union, Sherriff of Knottwood and Lord of the County of Areneld."

"Good boy," Prince William replied, tightening his grip on the boy's shoulder, "Now tell me: Am I fucking blind?"

The Messenger, wincing slightly in pain but trying his best to keep a stiff upper lip, replied in a wavering, quiet voice.

"No, your lordship?"

"Say it again, but not as a QUESTION." The Prince suddenly roared, spitting on the last syllable, saliva droplets landing on the window in front of them.

"No, your lordship!"

"GOOD BOY. So then why do you patronise me, child? Why do you run here and disturb me with useless trivia I have already fucking observed? Why are you here, you worthless stick?"

"It's my job, my lord…"

"IT'S MY JOB, MY LORD," the Prince screamed in a mocking, shrill screech, "IT'S MY JOB TO BE A SKINNY CHILD AND TELL PEOPLE THINGS THEY ALREADY KNOW! OH PLEASE FORGIVE ME MY LORD… Leave."

The boy nodded and backed away from the room in a hurried, scurrying shuffle that bordered on a curtsey. The Prince collapsed into his chair, staring out over the town.

"All of you. You stoic fucks standing like trees. Fetch me the Chief of the Guard. We have matters to discuss. And I don't want any children interrupting me. We're going to find the fucker that ruined my day."

# Chapter Six: The Night of Questions

It rained again that night, as it did most nights. It was a soft rain that began shortly after sunset, and it brought out all the snails from wherever they usually hide from the sun. They were most visible on white walls, like the ones outside the library. One particular wall was so pockmarked with snails that passers-by all huddled in raincoats and cosy under their umbrellas could scarcely tell the wall had ever been white to begin with. It was as though the snails belonged there. The snails were home, and the rain continued.

Marian sat alone in her house. It was a big house for one person to live in alone, but she liked it that way. There was plenty of storage space for her to keep anything and everything she might get her hands on, and the carpets were the perfect level of softness for one who walks around the house barefoot.

People rarely questioned the size of her house, or how she came to afford it. When they did, she told them she was a writer, and that she needed the space for "inspirational purposes", and that she bought the house with the proceeds from her latest novel. Sometimes, she would make up the plot of her latest novel. Her favourite of these lies was one she told to the butcher one morning in winter.

"It's about werewolves," she said with the utmost confidence, "But reverse ones. There's a pack of wolves that run around the forest, but every month at the full moon they come out into the city and run wild as humans. Then, the next morning, they wake up as wolves again."

There were no further questions, which Marian was almost insulted by. She had been so invested in her fake persona that she almost believed that she had actually written a novel about reverse werewolves.

At the moment, she was sat on the floor in front of her couch, the axe on her lap. She ran her fingers along the haft, up to the head, and lightly grazed the blade. Even with the gentlest touch, it was deathly sharp, leaving a noticeable scratch on the tip of her index finger. She picked it up in both hands, feeling its weight on her wrists and forearms, and slowly raised it up in the air, to see if she could.

It was almost unbearably heavy. She wasn't quite built for the majority of heavy lifting, and certainly not the kind of heavy lifting the headsman was accustomed to. She tried to keep it steady, but her arms began to shake and she gently brought it back down again. It had been fine carrying it from behind the tower to the graveyard as she had held it under one arm and gripped it tightly with the other hand, and looking back on the situation now, she imagined she had been working primarily on adrenaline.

She put the axe on the carpet, and then pulled it back into her lap. Dissatisfied, she put it under the couch, then pulled it back out again, then put it on top of the couch, then put it back on the carpet. She thought she was finally settled with it here, but then she moved through to her dining room and put it on the table instead. This was okay, up until she picked it back up and walked to her bedroom and put it under her bed.

Her room had the same soft carpet as the rest of the house, and many other soft things. Comparatively, the axe was probably sharper than all of the other items in the room combined. She had made her bed with two large quilts and eight pillows in a pile that almost looked like a nest, and at the foot of her bed she had an array of patterned cushions, all of which had been stolen from the seats in the library.

But no. No, this still wasn't the place to keep the axe. She tried all the rooms of her house, including the two bedrooms she never used, the kitchen, and the bathroom. Her house had one of the first fully functioning bathrooms in the city, and also a full-length mirror. She looked at herself, wearing her usual dark grey tunic with a black belt tied around the waist, and with pockets she had stitched in herself, with her black cowl, and brandishing an axe. It was a good look, all things considered, but she rather thought it would be more complete with her boots.

There was a knock at the door, and hurriedly, she laid the axe down on the bathroom floor. She rushed down the first few stairs, then gripped the bannisters on either side with both hands and swung the rest of the way down, a dangerous habit she'd had since childhood. She flung open the door, expecting Jemima, but stood in front of her were two of the city guards.

"We're sorry to disturb you, ma'am. We're just asking routine questions in light of a recent... Theft." said the one on the left.

"I suppose you've heard about it," added the one on the right, "Can we come in? It's pissing it down and there's about fifty snails just on your garden wall."

Reluctantly, Marian invited them in. They sat on the couch, and pulled down their mustard-coloured hoods, which matched the rest of their uniform. The one on the left pulled out a sheet of questions from their inside pocket.

"Where were you when the execution this morning took place?"

"I was there, watching."

"Can anybody verify that? Anyone else who lives here, maybe?"

"I live alone, but there's Priestess Trinna, she was up on the stage. She saw me. I was eating an apple."

"Right. Do you have a personal attachment to the man scheduled for execution this morning?"

Marian shook her head. It could have been almost anybody at the chopping block and she would've done the same thing.

"I see. Have you heard anybody talking about the events that took place today?"

Marian shook her head again.

"I came straight home," she spoke sincerely although it was not technically true, "I don't like noisy places, so I left when the crowd started getting too noisy."

"Alright. I think that's all the questions- as long as the Priestess can verify she saw you then that should be alright, I reckon... Sorry about this. We've asked everyone on this street. It's the most convenient street, you see- goes straight out of town on one end, and down to the docks on the other. Isn't that right?" he turned to the other guard.

"Yeah... Erm, this street's got them proper bathrooms though hasn't it? Hot running water and everything?" said the guard on the right. Marian's heart started pounding like a fist on a wooden door. She did her best to remain calm.

"Yes, it's fully functional," she said, "Just upstairs on the right."

Her palms began to sweat again. The guard nodded, stood, and walked upstairs. This was it. It was over, the game was up. She may as well go out fighting. She reached slowly for the pocket of her belted tunic to quickly grasp her dagger when the inevitable came, the guard discovering the headsman's axe lying on the floor, the unavoidable shouts and screams and fighting, more fighting, even more fighting than with Jemima earlier that day. It was coming, now, she could sense it. After a couple of minutes, finally, there was a voice.

"Oi," sounded the guard from upstairs, "That's not right, is it?"

The other guard, still on the couch, shouted back. "What's the matter?"

Here it was. The moment. It was so predictable, so obvious. She couldn't believe she'd left the axe on the bathroom floor. What was she thinking?

"Ma'am, I thought you said you lived alone?" the guard upstairs questioned.

That wasn't quite what Marian expected.

"... Yes, I do?" a quiver in her voice, her intonation raised just a little too highly.

"Then who's this girl sleeping?"

Jemima was in one of the bedrooms Marian never used, curled up on the bed, snoring casually. Marian didn't see her from downstairs, but knew who it must be.

"That's... My... Girlfriend?" Marian improvised, "She's... Staying the night."

There was a pause, and a creak of a floorboard as the guard stepped away.

"Oh. Alright, sorry about that."

He started coming down the stairs, mumbling something about being glad not to have woken her. Both of the guards pulled up their hoods, the one on the left pocketing the list of questions, and finally, after the most anxious visit of Marian's life, left to speak to somebody else.

Marian slowly turned away from the front door and looked up at the top of the stairs. And there she was- Jemima.

"Sorry, came in through the back way when I saw the guards. Good job I did though! I moved the axe for you- I mean, who leaves an axe in the bathroom?" She laughed.

Marian held back a laugh, pretending to not see any humour in the situation. "You broke in again?" she asked, folding her arms. Jemima folded her arms in response.

"Well yes! I had to, because I don't have a key, even though I'm your girlfriend..." She laughed again. This time, Marian couldn't hold back a laugh. The whole situation was just ridiculous- this woman, a woman she had only met earlier that day, had saved her from being arrested, but if it weren't for her then the series of events which lead to the near arrest might not have happened anyway. And now, here she was, ready to take Marian to the forest to meet other thieves.

Marian realised she had been thinking all of this while staring in half-focus at Jemima as she walked down the stairs. Before she realised it, Jemima was stood only a few inches in front of her, and it brought Marian back to reality with a slight jump, which was met with a smirk from Jemima.

"Are you ready?" Jemima whispered.

"I'm still not sure what it is I'm supposed to be ready for," Marian replied, "As I asked you to explain later."

"Well, how about I explain on the way?" Jemima smiled, before pulling up her hood, "Do you want to go through the back door or the front? If we go through the back, nobody will see us, but the front... The guards might think we're on a date."

Marian pulled down a large coat from a hook in the hallway, and they left through the front door, hoods up, Jemima walking slightly ahead, up the cobblestone road to the edge of town, and into Shorebark Forest.

## Chapter Seven: The Golden Arrow

Under the cover of the leaves, the rain barely reached them as they walked a well-trodden path through the woods.

"So," Jemima explained, "We're going to the tavern. We call it The Golden Arrow, I think- the name changes a lot."

"There's a tavern in the woods?" Marian asked, sceptical.

"Of course! Where are the really downtrodden folk going to drink otherwise? The Intoxicated Swan? Or that bar down by the docks, Rickman's Rope? No, and no. Those places are all for show. They give the impression that they're for us, the common people, but really they're all run by the richest people in town. Pure theft, is what it is."

"I suppose that's true," Muttered Marian, pushing brambles away from her face, "But what makes this one so different? How do you know it's not for show?"

"We know it isn't because it is!"

Rain fell on leaves, and leather boots crunched on stones and dry pieces of bark, and neither one said anything for a good ten seconds.

"I'm sorry, what?" Marian finally said, understandably confused.

"It'll make sense when we get there. The point is, we don't make any secrets about our secrets- it's sort of charming in how we're very open about the fact that the tavern is a total front for a secret crime cult."

"A *cult?*"

"Sorry. A *council.*"

"So why did you say cult?"

"It just sort of rolls off the tongue. It's easy to say, you can greet people with a simple hello! We're the all-female thief cult!"

"So it's all women?"

"Yes! Well, the Council is. The Hooded Council."

"Wow. Okay. Can we start from the beginning again? I'm getting extremely confused back here. I almost just fell in a pond, too."

Jemima laughed to herself. They had reached an old, rusted gate connected to a broken fence that ran off into the forest, into darker holes where the light of the moon could not reach. It seemed impossible- as though it were only standing up through continued prayer, or consistent luck. Jemima flicked a latch on the opposite side and opened it with a creak.

"Alright," she said, "In this tavern, poor people meet nightly. The ale's free, the food's free, the heat and the shelter are free- and it's free because we steal it. I'm part of the Hooded Council, we're a group of seven women who maintain the upkeep of the bar so that everybody who deserves to be happy and warm… Can be happy and warm!"

"So why are you bringing me here?"

"I've been sort of testing you," she said, trying to get a sturdy footing on a slope that tumbled downwards somewhat dangerously, especially in the dark, "To see if you'd be good enough to join the Council!"

Marian thought this over. On one hand, she had always worked alone, slipping away from crowds and stealing things for her own benefit. On the other hand, living in such a large house alone had gotten quite monotonous. And though the past days and nights had been terrifying, and had scared Marian in ways she had never been scared before, she was intrigued by this new development, this glimpse of the sky in an otherwise overcast year.

They managed to get down the slope without incident, and there it was. The Golden Arrow, in all its glory- bigger than Marian had expected, and warmer. The lantern lights outside came into focus, one of them swinging carelessly, shifting its glow over the sign and the ground. From inside came occasional shouts of happiness, and what Marian thought to be the sound of a dropped plate followed by a crowd cheering. There were a lot of snails on the walls. She stood, staring, still bewildered by this sudden building deep within the woods, as Jemima walked to the door, and then turned back to face Marian.

"It's not too late to go home," she said sweetly, "If it's too much, you can go, and I won't bother you again. But if you want to come in, then... You're welcome."

Marian made eye contact with Jemima, who had one hand on the door and the other stretched out towards her, gesturing for her to hold her hand. The corners of Marian's mouth twitched as she slid her hand into Jemima's, and Jemima pushed open the door.

It was green. The first thing Marian noticed was that it was very, very green. The walls were painted green, the decoration on the chairs was green, even the mugs of ale were green. People were sat at round tables laughing and drinking, people were stood at the bar making lazy gossip with each other, and in one corner, a bard holding a lute was playing the last few notes of a song, for which everyone cheered.

"And now, a song close to all of our hearts- The tale of Robin Hood!" the bard exclaimed, flipping shoulder-length blonde hair out of his eyes as some people clapped and others simply raised their mugs.

The bard began singing.

"Listen, all ye gentlemen,
and ladies listen good,
I tell you all a story now,
the tale of Robin Hood!
Never has an archer lived,
with hands so swift or aim so true,
And never a better thief than Hood!
A blackguard through and through!
His dagger sharper than his wits,
A coat of brilliant green,
He steals from the rich! Gives to the poor!
The greatest man you've ever seen!"

The crowd, including Jemima, cheered. Marian was still getting used to the overwhelming smell of alcohol. The song carried on, talking about Robin's various valiant deeds, of his noble thievery from the rich, of the entire legend of this man named Robin Hood. Marian wondered if she'd ever get to meet him. She turned to ask Jemima about this, and only then realised that they were still holding hands.

When the song ended, Jemima smiled widely at Marian and lead her through the room, nodding and waving at people sitting down, a lot of whom were entirely fixated on Marian.

"Why are they staring?" Marian whispered.

"Oh, just because you're new," Jemima reassured her with a gentle squeeze of her hand, "They'll stop that soon, I promise."

They reached a back door, and Jemima took a key from her belt to open it.

"Sorry, could you just wait here?" she asked, suddenly bashful, "I've just... I've sort of got to ask if it's okay for you to come in."

Marian glanced around at the crowd. None of them seemed to be staring right now. She nodded in response, and Jemima nodded too before going into the room.

It was thirty seconds at most, but it felt like longer. Marian tried to take in as much of the tavern as possible- the bard still playing his songs, the odour of ale becoming gradually more tolerable but the taste of it in the air lingering on her tongue, the lovely shade of green so many things seemed to be painted. A man brushed past her on his way to speak to the bard, and she shivered at the contact, which he seemed to not notice. Finally, Jemima opened the door again, and gently pulled Marian inside.

It was darker in here, but still noticeably green. There was a round table with seven chairs, two of which were currently occupied. At the far end of the table sat an older woman, and to her right, a woman in approximately her forties.

"Hello." The older woman said, almost too softly to hear over the background noise of the Golden Arrow. The younger of the two women said nothing, but stared and seemed to silently judge.

"Celinda, Deryn- this is Marian!" Jemima announced as though showing off.

The older woman stood and approached Marian, inspecting her features and her stature. Marian was determined not to budge, though the situation became ever more intimidating. Marian took in every line and wrinkle on the older woman's face, the bags under her eyes- her eyes which still shone bright blue, even now.

"Yes," the woman said, "This is Marian."

She turned to Jemima.

"I'd like to speak to her in private. Would you go and give the bard a telling off? Specifically mention the difference between "well" and "good". Keep him quiet for a while."

"Yes, Celinda!" Jemima nodded and left the room. Marian stood, exposed, in front of the older woman- now identified as Celinda.

Celinda looked deep into Marian's eyes, almost looking past them at something only she could see. She squinted slightly. Marian's eyes began to water but she felt that if she were to blink, she would fail an unspoken test. After another miniature eternity, Celinda spoke again.

"What are you here for?" She asked.

Marian stammered over her words, her eyes stinging. She blinked several times in quick succession.

"I'm here- I'm here because... I was curious."

"That's not true. Tell me the truth."

Marian took a step back, and Celinda's gaze did not falter. At the table, Deryn watched the events in passive but solid stillness.

"Tell me the truth," Celinda repeated, "About why you came here."

Marian met Celinda's stare again, and furrowed her brow.

"I came here to do something good."

"Rhywbeth yn dda." Celinda said over her shoulder, addressing Deryn. Marian didn't recognise the language.

"Yna gadewch iddi." Deryn replied. Marian rather felt as though she was missing out on a secret, which she didn't like. She loved knowing secrets, and was very good at keeping them.

"Ie," Celinda smiled, then turned back to Marian, "Yes. Yes, I can see this working... When the other members of the Council arrive, we'll have a proper introduction, hm?"

The noise of the tavern began to increase in volume as the bard sang a new song. People cheered and raised their drinks once more, and as she took a seat at the round table, Marian's cheeks flushed with the particular brand of happiness that comes from finding your place.

"Will I get to meet Robin Hood?" Marian asked, but Celinda only laughed.

## Chapter Eight: The Knight and the Priestess

The kettle rumbled seductively.

Sir Patton Cross had left his boots by the door, and hung a new hat on the hat stand. He'd rather expected to die today, but evidently he had been given a second chance. He was sat in the house behind the Church. Priestess Trinna insisted he come here, to receive blessings, a warm meal, and to hide from anybody who might try to harass him at his own house. Trinna was, at that moment, preparing tea.

She settled their cups down on the table, and they sipped their drinks in peace. It was a lovely house, Patton thought. Just an absolutely beautiful little house.

They exchanged small tales of their lives. Neither of them had laughed this much in longer than they could ever remember. They told old jokes, anecdotes from days gone by, and discussed their individual plans for the future. Patton hadn't been aware he had plans for the future, but when he began to speak, the floodgates opened and the ideas seemed to form themselves in front of them.

He described wanting a house on the beach. A proper beach, not like the one outside Knottwood. One back in the southern reaches of the country. Knottwood beach was all pebbles and discomfort, and there was rarely a day sunny enough that the light would blind you to its ugliness. He described comfort. A new chair, a soft bed, a warm blanket, money for upkeep. He described his dream house as a wooden hut, with several windows that could overlook the sea.

"The sea down south is different," he explained, "It's warmer, and so is the sand."

He spoke of gold grains underfoot, and picking up shells. He still had one shell, one particular shell that he picked up as a child. He kept it in a box in a drawer so as not to lose it, or damage it. It wasn't that it was a particularly rare looking shell- in fact, it looked the same as most other shells. When one thinks of a seashell, the image that is conjured is precisely how this shell looked. It wasn't the appearance of the seashell that attracted him to it- it was its location.

Amongst the sheet of shining sunglow, thousands of shells were scattered, if not millions. Barely a step could be walked without stepping on several. But this shell wasn't in the sand. There was a lone rock, near no other rocks. It seemed almost out of place- like there ought to be another rock nearby, or next to it, or on top of it. But no- on top of it was a shell. A single shell sat stationary in a small dip, and Patton took it.

Something about its position made it special. It seemed like shell royalty. If shells had a hierarchy, this one would be at the top, its throne of stone raising it high above all shells who dared oppose it. Or, at least, that is what Patton thought as a child. Now it was an object of purely sentimental value.

They were so wrapped up in their comfortable conversation that they didn't hear the first knock on the door.

They heard the second knock, but weren't sure if it was the door or just the wind. They were silent, for a moment, and then there was a third knock. Leaving Patton at the table, Trinna went to welcome the new guests.

There were two guards at the door. They were soaked through to their skin, and they trod their damp boots all over Trinna's floor.

"This is where you've been hiding is it?" said the one on the left to Patton. Patton tensed up, preparing himself for another arrest.

"Don't worry. We're not here for you this time. The way it works is, you showed up. You did everything you were meant to, right? Not your fault the axe was taken. That's all we're looking for." The one on the right reassured him. Trinna, nervously, offered them both tea, but they both shook their heads.

The guard on the left pulled out a list of questions, but the guard on the right nudged him and whispered something in his ear.

"Oh. Right. Priestess. Hello. First of all we've got to ask you- did you see Marian Stoke at the execution? She lives up the road to the docks."

Trinna began to fluster, and offered them tea again, but they just insisted she answer the question.

"Yes. Yes I saw her. She was... Eating an *apple*, as I recall." Trinna said, stuttering through the truth, panicked. She had been having a nice evening.

"Thank you, ma'am," said the guard on the right, "That matches up with what she was telling us."

The guard on the right looked back over at Patton, who was facing away, staring down at his tea. Trinna was still panicking. She felt the need to fill the silence. She knew she absolutely should not fill the silence.

She filled the silence.

"And the last time I saw Marian before this morning was last night when she was attempting to rob a grave," the words practically sprinting out of her mouth, tumbling over each other in a race to be first to be heard, "But I caught her in the act because another young woman told me it was happening," the words at full speed now like horses bolting free of their carriages, "And I told her I wouldn't tell the guards if she left but I'm telling you now because I'm awful, I'm absolutely awful and my tea's going cold and you've tracked mud all over my carpet and," she breathed in, a temporary moment of relief, "I'm sorry but I had to tell you the truth."

There was an awkward lull. Patton had slowly turned to face Trinna. The guards had slowly turned to face each other.

"I think perhaps..." said the one on the left.

"We'll be needing an arrest warrant." Finished the one on the right.

They dragged their filthy boots back out of Trinna's house, and Trinna began to cry. Patton leapt from his seat and held her by the shoulders.

"It's- It's okay, Trinna. You did the right thing, you had to turn her in."

"NO, Patton, it isn't," she sobbed, "Because I TOLD her to do something GOOD, and now I've gone and ruined it."

"What do you mean?"

Trinna wiped her eyes and looked into Patton's.

"I just... Do you think, that- maybe, after I told her that...? She stole the axe?"

Deep in the forest, four hooded figures approached the tavern. The rain was harder now, and was forcing itself through the cover of leaves, so the people in the woods pulled their hoods down further, and their coats tighter. A squirrel scurried by, seeking any kind of shelter it could find from the brittle waterfall. The only ones not attempting to cover up where the snails, who were truly out in full force now.

Almost every surface was covered in snails. Their origin was a mystery- where had they been hiding before the rain, exactly? How were there so many of them? The woman leading the pack of companions theorised that maybe they fell in the raindrops. It was a nice notion that she entertained herself with as she pushed away brambles and tried to avoid falling in small ponds that barely surpassed the title of "puddle", until she began to think about it more. The prospect of every individual raindrop potentially housing a snail was too much. Snails are a good idea, she thought, but there is a *limit*.

Through a rusted gate and down a dangerous slope, they arrived at The Golden Arrow, and forced their way through the crowd inside. The fourth in the single row of people in hoods grabbed Jemima by her forearm and pulled her along with them, and the first in the line opened the back door to the room with the round table.

Marian turned to face them as they marched in.

"Hello," she said, "I'm Marian, and I'm..."

"Sitting in my seat." Interrupted one of the newcomers to the room, pulling off her hood. She was a darker black than Marian, and her eyes were darker, but her head was completely shaved. The hood she pulled down was a deep emerald green, as was the coat it was attached to. Her tone was harsh, and Marian was unsure whether it was a joke or not.

"I'm sorry, I'll..." Marian began, but was interrupted again.

"Now, now- settle, ladies." Celinda gave a small wave of her hand to Jemima, who nodded and rushed out of the room. Everybody sat down, including the woman from whom Marian had apparently stolen a seat. The woman winked.

Jemima rushed back into the room holding a chair, and the other women budged over to let her into the circle, where she sat across from Marian.

"I believe introductions are in order," Celinda announced, resting her palms on the table, "Everybody- this is Marian, Marian Stoke. She is the one we have been discussing- the grave robber."

There was a murmur of recognition and a bright smile from Jemima.

"She has proven herself worthy to join us... Almost. Very nearly. We're going to have to put her through just a little bit more- sorry, dear- before she's completely ready."

Marian looked from face to face frantically, unaware that there were more tests.

"And now, let us introduce ourselves to her. As you know, Marian, my name is Celinda, and you have met Deryn and Jemima already."

Jemima waved her hand in an unnecessary greeting. Deryn did nothing.

"Now, the others. These ladies will be your new friends, I'm sure- we have Xiang, Aleta, Paloma who happens to be Aleta's daughter, and Quilla, who knows full well that having an assigned seat at a round table is senseless and redundant." Celinda concluded with a knowing smile.

As she listed the names, Marian tried to take in the specifics of their appearances. They all wore the same green hooded coat, all of which were saturated with rain water, but that was where the similarities ended.

Xiang was pale, and had winged her eyes with perhaps the most flawlessly applied makeup Marian had ever seen. She had short, straight black hair that fell just below her ears, her nose was short and wide, and her lips were painted the pink of raspberries

Aleta was undoubtedly Mediterranean- Marian wondered briefly whether her and her daughter might be related to the Lords and Ladies of the expanding Mediterranean Empire- and had eyes almost the same green as her coat. Her hair was tied back into a tight, low ponytail.

Paloma resembled her mother in most features- they had the same eyes in shape and colour, the same low eyebrow arch, even the same lip shape- but Poloma's hair was loose, curled, and unnaturally red.

Marian had already taken in Quilla's features, but looked again anyway, and noticed her eye makeup was as beautifully applied as Xiang's. Marian made a mental note to ask one of them where they learned how to do that at the next available opportunity.

She then glanced over at Deryn- she was white, and blonde, with cropped hair, and in fact looked incredibly like how she imagined a younger Priestess Trinna would look, as though they were cousins, or perhaps even sisters.

Finally, she looked at Jemima, and Jemima was looking back. Marian looked away, hastily, blushing slightly at being caught- unaware that Jemima was also blushing for exactly the same reasons.

Marian tuned back into the conversation.

"Now- in terms of her test. We are all, of course, painfully aware that the King's brother is currently staying at the tower…" Celinda began.

The women around the table, including Marian, gave a collective grumble. They'd all heard of the King's brother. Whenever the King was away, his brother assumed command of the country and introduced the most ridiculous laws imaginable, only for them to be wiped away with a single wave of the King's hand upon his return- though the damage the punishments for breaking these laws inflicted could and would never be forgotten.

"… And so, therefore, is his crown," she continued, "His gaudy, tacky, absurd excuse for a crown that resembles a hat my grandfather used to wear, but infinitely more bejewelled. It isn't the hat we're interested in, of course- it is the aforementioned jewels, dears."

Marian had begun to understand where this was going.

"I have been considering this for some time- who would be best for this job? I have wondered. Who has the skills? I have pondered. Who has the strength of stomach to look at this absolutely ridiculous hat without becoming violently ill? Is a question I have laboured over long into many nights. And I think, ladies, we have found our answer. We have found our thief."

Everybody turned to Marian.

"Here we have a girl- a young woman- who stole a headsman's axe without being caught. Who- from what I hear- can steal a man's hat from his head without him noticing."

"To be fair, he was very drunk…" Marian said. She stopped talking when Celinda raised her hand.

"Here we have one who robs from graves without flinching. She is the perfect candidate, is she not, to break into the tower and steal the Prince's garish crown?"

Marian watched everybody nod. Deryn nodded, but not Quilla.

"The only thing I've seen her steal is my seat. Where IS this axe anyway?"

Jemima turned, suddenly snapping.

"It's in her house. It's under one of the beds, in the bedroom just next to the bathroom. I saw it. I put it there. Do you not believe it's there?" Jemima questioned.

"I won't believe it until I've seen it." Quilla replied.

"Then *go and see it*." Jemima hissed.

"This," Celinda interrupted with the tone of one trying to attract attention to break up a fight, "Brings us on to the next point. The axe is still in Marian's house, unguarded and alone. Somebody ought to go and get it, don't you think?"

Everybody nodded. Including Deryn, again. Marian wondered why that was. It seemed Deryn understood the language they all spoke in but refused to speak in it herself. This time, Quilla nodded too.

"I will." She said.

Celinda's lips curled into what might have been a smile.

"You will, that's correct."

Celinda turned to Deryn.

"Beth ydych chi'n feddwl?" Celinda asked.

""Mae hi'n perthyn yma." Deryn stated with a slow nod.

There was that language again. Marian desperately wanted to know what they were saying. It sounded familiar, but she couldn't place it, like the face of an old acquaintance.

She realised that probably wasn't the most important thing to be thinking about. Jewels were fine- she had taken necklaces, rings, earrings, adornments of all descriptions from graves and market stalls. Hats were fine- she had recently, of course, taken a hat just to see if she could. The tower was, in theory, fine- or at least the area behind it was, the unguarded yard.

The tower was guarded, and that was what worried her. The guards.

The guards who had visited Trinna's house were on their way back to the guard barracks, walking once more through the rain. The rain was slowing now, nearing its finishing point, but by this point they'd stopped caring. They couldn't get more drenched than they already were.

"Do you reckon though," said the guard on the left, "That we actually need a warrant?"

"What d'you mean?" asked the guard on the right.

"I mean can't we just show up there? We've been told to ask questions, to speak to everyone on this road. Why can't we just nip round there again, knock on the door, and arrest her?"

"Well because how are the other guards going to feel about that? We show up like "Oh we didn't find who stole the axe but the Priestess said she found somebody robbing a grave so we arrested that person"? We need to let them know beforehand, that's why we need a warrant."

"Oh. But that's... That's going to take ages."

"You're joking right? Why is that an issue?"

"We have to walk all the way there, probably wake up the Chief of the Guard by now, get him to write and sign a warrant, then come back out here, walk all the way down the road, knock on the door and probably wake up the girl by now, then arrest her, and walk all the way back up the road."

"Oh. I see what you're saying."

"Yes."

"But the problem is…"

"Oh no."

"The problem is that we're guards. This is our job. We've got to arrest her! What if she robs a grave again tonight?"

"But would she? Would she rob one now? Now that the Priestess caught her?"

"The criminal always returns to the scene…"

"Oh, don't. The amount of fucking times I've heard that… Fine. Let's go get a warrant. We can at least pick up some umbrellas while we're there. Why didn't we bring them out anyway?"

"We didn't know the rain would be this bad."

"The rain's always this bad."

"Then because we're fools."

"Which is why we're guards in the first place."

They laughed because they needed to, and Trinna ran from her house.

## Chapter Nine: Thick as Thieves

Coming out of the forest was much harder than coming in.

Marian had always found coming out difficult- generally, she arrived at a graveyard unencumbered and left with pockets or satchels full of coin and jewels, which made concealment much more difficult. It was of course also tremendously easy to walk into a shop with the intent of stealing, but immensely more of a problem to come out of one with a loaf of bread tucked under her arm. Perhaps most difficult of all had been coming out to her family the day she told them she was their daughter and their sister, as opposed to the son and brother they had previously been lead to believe she was.

That had been an odd sort of day. At the time, her name had not been Marian. She was midway through her teens, and hadn't had a haircut in about a year and a half. It had grown upwards and outwards, and was naturally tightly curled, and she loved it. She also loved her lip makeup, having found the perfect shade at a market stall that day. "Found", of course, being the operative word, as she had no intention of paying for it when she discovered it, though now she realised how well it complimented her skin tone, she thought she might well consider purchasing it legally next time. Shortly after stealing it, she had run into a few friends- or rather, acquaintances, as she found friends to often be too difficult- who showed her their own purchases, and then wouldn't let the conversation switch until she told them what she'd bought, so she showed them the lip paint.

They didn't respond well to the lip paint. In their opinion, she ought not to be wearing it. In their opinion, she was breaking some sort of abstract unwritten rule by even owning it. In their opinion, she was a boy, and in their opinion, boys should not wear lipstick.

She had been keeping the fact that she was not a boy secret for quite some time at that point, and it had become too much of a weight to bear, too much of a hindrance, too big of a story not to tell. In the end, being told by people she was relatively sure she was at least a little bit fond of that she shouldn't wear something that she thought would make her feel more comfortable was the tipping point.

She shouted in their unsuspecting faces, hurling away the burden of muteness she had been carrying on her shoulders. She shouted that she was a girl, not a boy. She shouted that even if she were a boy, which she definitely wasn't, that they should respect her choices nonetheless. She shouted that something as arbitrary as the colour somebody paints their lips shouldn't matter to them at all, that she wasn't hurting anybody by doing it, and that once more, she was a girl. She shouted that she was doing it for herself, not for them, and that it was her life and not theirs, and that she would wear whatever colour lip paint she felt like she ought to be wearing.

She shouted, and people heard, and she ran. She ran all the way home, and up to her room, where she sat in front of a mirror and painted her lips. She changed out of the clothes she was wearing and into a black layered tunic dress, with a green floral pattern. She made sure her hair was as big as possible. She coated a strip of paper in a wax substance she'd stolen several days prior, placed it on her chin and wrenched it away, pulling any residual hairs that may have grown there away. She laced up her boots and stomped down the stairs into the family room of her house, and she waited.

She waited for her family to come home. Her siblings came first, and saw her stood there in the dress she had been longing to wear for weeks. Her mother came later, and saw her daughter stood there, finally stood in the way she had wanted her family to see her.

She stood there, open and out as the girl she knew she was, and she couldn't think of a single word to explain. She'd thought this moment over a thousand times. She had imagined sitting her family down after dinner, when nobody had any pressing engagements, and telling them frankly and openly about how she knew herself, and that it wasn't a choice she'd made, it was just how she was, and that she hoped they would accept it. She didn't imagine it like this. She didn't imagine that she'd be so determined to tell them before word spread around the streets and found its way back here that she forgot any possible way of talking about it.

Eventually, she told them.

Her brothers didn't understand why she couldn't be a boy any more.

Her sisters didn't understand why she suddenly "wanted" to be a girl.

Her mother didn't say anything.

Marian left the room.

Later, Marian left a note. Later still, Marian left the house. Soon after, Marian left the town. She packed as many bags as possible with warm clothes and changes of shoes, left her home, and travelled, eventually arriving at Knottwood.

Along the way, she was asked her name, and she told them it was Marian Stoke.

Marian Stoke finally got out of the forest. The hillock she'd had to slightly stumble down to reach the tavern was practically torture on the way up, especially after the rain. She thought this was probably a test- anybody who could stand knowing they had to walk back through the forest after a visit to the tavern was probably strong-willed enough to become a regular visitor. The gate remained as rusted as ever. She admired its steady resolve.

As she walked down the cobblestone road between the docks and the edge of town, she watched snails slowly make their retreat into wherever they usually hid. She passed her house, and then the tavern the drunk man had stumbled from, and for the first time, saw the sign- "The Intoxicated Swan". She remembered Jemima mentioning that name earlier, but she'd never known this specific tavern was called that, having never looked in its direction during the day and being more interested in the people pouring out of it during the night. It sounded busy, but not as busy as the Golden Arrow had been.

It was late now, at a time when she'd usually be preparing to go to the graveyard. As she passed it, she wondered for a moment if she had the time to quickly rob a grave on the way, but then noticed the lights were on in Trinna's house behind the church and thought better of it. She stepped over a snail which looked as though it was having a harder time than the other snails in getting home.

She hadn't walked much further when she heard hurried steps behind her. Her heart rate increased ever so slightly as she quickened her pace, only for the steps to become faster too. Just as she noticed the shadow of somebody close behind cast near to her and she began to run, the person in pursuit fell, thudding onto the ground and making a shocked, pained sound in a familiar voice.

Marian turned for the first time since leaving the tavern, and saw Jemima lying on the ground, pushing herself up.

"Jemima? What... Did you slip?"

"No," Jemima said, panting and gasping for breath, finally pushing herself up on wet, muddy hands and standing up as straight as she possibly could, "I... I jumped over a snail, I didn't want to crush it."

"You *jumped?*" Marian tried not to laugh.

"Yes, I jumped! I've been following you but you walk so fast, and I had to run, and I'd fallen over twice already but I just didn't want to hurt the snail, alright?"

Marian was really struggling to hold in her laughter. "I mean... I get it, nobody wants to hurt a snail, but I didn't think you'd be that clumsy- you seemed rather dextrous this morning."

"That was different, that was self-defence, sort of," Jemima explained, not as exasperated now she'd had time to catch her breath, "And there weren't any snails in your house."

"Fair enough," Marian admitted, storing her laughter away for now, keeping it for later in case something funnier happened, "But why were you following me in the first place? Is this just what you do, you stalk me for fun every night?"

Jemima looked hurt, and wiped her hands on the side of her coat.

"I thought you might want help, in... In getting into the tower."

"Oh."

Marian swelled up with guilt, which manifested in her cheeks. Any emotion that made her cheeks glow red annoyed her. They gave the whole game away.

"I didn't mean to be rude… I was trying to make a joke," Marian said, stepping toward her in an attempt at reassurance, "I'm glad you're here. And I'm glad the snail's still here too."

Jemima laughed just a little, then straightened up.

"Shall we go, then?" She asked, and Marian nodded happily.

They walked on for a while, their steps falling into sync over time. It was perhaps a little more casual than either of them had expected considering their destination. They didn't speak, and the only things breaking the silence were their feet on the road. It was a nice silence, a comfortable silence, the silence of two people who have known each other for a long time, though of course, they had not.

They turned onto a road that led more directly to the centre of town, and began to talk again.

"This is the road I ran down," Marian said, "After I stole the axe."

Jemima looked around. It was a narrower road than, with taller buildings.

"Is this… Rodney Street? Quilla and I got an amazing load here one night a couple of years ago, at number sixty-five. It's full of offices, but the attic is full of antiques… Or rather, WAS full of antiques…"

"Does Quilla dislike me?" Marian asked.

"What?"

"Does she not like me? She didn't seem overly fond of me at the Golden Arrow. Have I offended her?"

"Oh, no! She's like that with almost everybody, I wouldn't take it personally. It can get a little frustrating, but ultimately she's… Good at what she does."

Marian nodded. She quickly became aware that Jemima was actually looking forward and wouldn't see her nod.

"Okay." Marian said.

They turned a sharp corner.

"I wish I'd known." Marian said, almost mournfully.

"Known?"

"About you. About all of you," she elaborated, "It would have been…"

She let the sentence trail off. Above the tall buildings, the tower was coming into view, a monolith against a starry sky, lit by lanterns and the distant moon. At the very top, the lone window glowed with a faint gradient from blue to orange. Jemima and Marian said nothing, and Jemima squeezed Marian's hand reassuringly.

Up until that point, Marian hadn't realised they were holding hands.

Clinging to the side of the buildings, hugging the shadows, they slowly approached the town square together, and the plan became obvious to both of them as they hastily whispered it almost in perfect synchronisation.

The front entrance would be guarded, as it always was when a noble was visiting. The back entrance, by the yard, would be guarded tonight to prevent further thefts after the axe fiasco. The guards at the front would not be allowed to leave their station unless an altercation began in the town square, or until they changed shifts with other guards who would currently be resting in the barracks on the other side of the square. The guards at the back would be poised to pounce on any threat, having always been told that the criminal returns to the scene of the crime.

The plan was to sneak through the back entrance.

Marian would sneak behind a row of houses next to the tower, and hide behind the fence separating the alley from the yard. Jemima would run from the street they currently stood in and put on a dramatic display of screaming and almost falling into the fountain so the guards at the front entrance had to rush to her and investigate. She would tell them somebody had been chasing her, and point in the direction of the graveyard. The front guards would call to the guards at the back entrance who would need to deal with the threat of the person giving chase to Jemima while the front guards told her to go and speak to other guards in the barracks about the attacker and then return to their positions at the entrance.

At this point, while the back guards were away, Marian would sneak in the back entrance, and gradually make her way up to the top of the tower and into the Prince's bedroom, posing as a servant in case he awoke. Provided he did not, she would steal the crown and leave, back through the back entrance, still unguarded, if done swiftly enough.

It began as planned.

Marian slipped into the thin alleyway behind the houses and, with hardly a sound, floated through like an errant dandelion seed.

Jemima lurched herself into the town square, and screamed, a shrill cry echoing off the walls, even louder than the rushing water of the fountain, which she fell towards in a pantomime pratfall, landing sideways on the ground, facing away from the tower.

The guards sprinted over to her, one of them holding a torch.

"Are you okay, miss?" the one with the torch inquired.

Jemima began to cry. "I... I was being... I was being chased, and he, he, he went towards the graveyard, he was, holding an axe..."

"An *axe*?" repeated the one without the torch. "Bloody hell- HEY, YOU TWO AT THE BACK- WE'VE GOT A RUNNER, POSSIBLY WITH CONTRABAND."

As the two guards at the front tried to pick up Jemima and assure her of her safety as long as she went to the barracks, the two guards at the back ran around the tower and gave chase to an imaginary assailant.

Marian leapt over the fence, landing softly, and simply walked in the back door.

She was in a small corridor now that led to the main chamber at the bottom of the tower, where there was a spiral staircase that lead to the very top of the tower. Along the way were windowless rooms where members of the city court would currently be sleeping, and in a small room about halfway up, the servants would be sleeping too.

Marian slithered through the door at the end of the corridor and started up the staircase, so delicately she practically did it almost without making contact with the floor.

Outside, Jemima staggered to the barracks. The plan here was to carry on with the story of an assailant wielding an axe, so that when the theft of the crown was discovered, they would blame this mystery man.

She entered the barracks.

Priestess Trinna turned to face her.

Inside the tower, Marian dashed up the stairs, being careful to tread lightly to avoid any that would creak. Her heart thumped relentlessly like a spectator in a crowd pumping their fist to encourage her to keep going. Then, immediately slowing her pace and trying to stick to short, quiet breaths, she entered the servants' quarters.

As expected, the servants were all sleeping, which meant the Prince would be too. That made things easier. She took one of their uniforms, which was simple, plain black, removed her coat, and wore the uniform over her clothes. She left the room as quickly as she came in, dropped her coat by the door, and continued up the stairs.

She arrived outside the room at the top, and listened for a moment. Silence. Anxious silence, but silence.

She opened the door. Two lamps by the window cast shadows of the Prince's chair that overlapped and mirrored each other on the carpet. On the walls hung similar pictures of the ocean to the ones Marian had had little time to look at on the way up. On the left were shelves of books, a table with a deep blue tablecloth, and a chair on either side. On the right was another door, the only barrier between this room and the room in which the Prince slept.

"*What are you doing here?*" Trinna whispered angrily to Jemima, back at the guard barracks.

"I- I'm..." Jemima failed to reply, baffled.

*"I'm trying to convince them there was no grave robbery, that I dreamt it,"* Trinna said through gritted teeth, *"Because they're going to put an arrest warrant out for..."*

Two guards walked down the stairs in single file, then stood next to each other in front of Trinna and Jemima.

Jemima's stomach sank as she realised the risk this posed. If these two guards arrest Marian tonight, they'll find her with the crown, and then...

"Who's this then?" asked the guard on the left.

"Oi," answered the guard on the right, "I know her! Marian's girlfriend, right?"

Trinna turned and squinted at Jemima. *Girlfriend?*

"I... Yes," Jemima said, "And I've... I've been attacked. Outside."

"Then that explains..." the guard on the left said to the guard on the right.

"The screaming, yeah?" the guard on the right said to the guard on the left.

"Yes... That was me."

"Blimey. Busy night..." Muttered the guard on the left, "Well we'll be right with you, miss. We're just trying to sort something out here. So you're saying you dreamt the events of the night in question, Priestess."

Trinna nodded, steadfast.

"Right... Because you know, if you're lying now and we find out there was actually a robbery, you can get prosecuted for harbouring a fugitive, technically? Wouldn't help your case that old Patton Cross is your boyfriend now."

Jemima looked up and squinted at Trinna. *Boyfriend?*

Trinna nodded again, unwavering and absolute.

Marian opened the door to the bedroom. It was dark, the only light coming from the lamps in the windowed room. She took in as many details as possible in case she ever needed to come back.

There was a four-poster bed adorned in what seemed to be an even darker blue than the paintings outside. There were paintings in here too, one of a large shipwreck and the other of, from what Marian could tell, a mermaid wielding an anchor-shaped dagger. Marian checked her pockets for her own dagger, and realised she had left it in her coat downstairs. She panicked for a moment.

No, she thought, panicking won't help. What good will panicking do? Let's get the crown and get out.

And there it was. On a nightstand, next to the sleeping form of the Prince, his large chest moving with his breaths like the tide on a shore, was the crown, in all its obnoxious glory.

She crept over to it. Predictably, a floorboard creaked, but the Prince did not awaken. Over years of thievery Marian had begun to suspect that people with valuables to hide intentionally installed creaky floorboards near their beds.

She took the crown. It was hers. She held it in her hands like a mother holding a child, and she hastened out of the room as silently as possible.

"I understand. But he's not my boyfriend. He's a house guest." Trinna explained.

The guard on the right smiled. "Whatever you say, Priestess... We just hope you're keeping the faith."

Trinna gave a sarcastic smile.

"Anyway..." the guard on the left stood forward and addressed Jemima, "The person who attacked you."

"A man. He ran towards the graveyard." Jemima said, pulse racing.

The guards turned to each other. The one on the right sighed.

"Are you sure it wasn't a dream? I don't want to have to walk all the way back down there…"

"It wasn't a dream," she said, "He definitely attacked me, and he had an axe, and I ran to the town square, and…"

"*He had an axe?*" The guards said in unison, then looked at each other again, and the one on the left immediately ran out. The one on the right followed, but stopped, picked up a sword from a rack, and ran out after the one on the left.

Trinna and Jemima turned to face each other.

Aleta and Quilla turned to face each other.

"This is it? She actually did steal it?" Quilla asked.

"Yes, that's the one." Aleta replied.

"Fuck. It's like nothing, this is air, practically. You didn't have to come with me, I can lift this on my own."

"And what if you get caught." Aleta stated rather than asked, her voice monotone and her expression unchanging.

Quilla sighed. "Fine. Well, we've got it. Let's go. Back or front?"

"Front, I should think."

They left Marian's house through the front door, Quilla holding the headsman's axe under her arm.

"THERE," shouted a guard, "HE'S THERE, AND HE'S GOT ANOTHER WOMAN!"

The two guards from the back of the tower sprinted towards Aleta and Quilla.

The two guards running from the barracks quickened their pace.

Marian left the tower, threw off the servant's uniform, put on her coat and shoved the crown into a side pocket. She heard the shouts, and feared the worst.

Jemima and Trinna heard the shouts too, and ran outside.

The two guards from the back entrance ran after Aleta and Quilla as they tried to flee into the woods, and the guards from the barracks caught up. Marian slipped down connected back alleys and reached the edge of town just as Quilla passed the border between the town and the forest. The guard on the right was the fastest runner and caught up with Quilla, and slashed with his sword at her back.

Quilla screamed, and turned, hitting the guard with the handle of the axe and knocking him into a pond before staggering off into the forest, taking off her coat and holding it as well as she could against her back to stem the bleeding.

The other guards ran towards them. One of the guards from the back entrance knocked into Aleta, toppling her over, her head colliding with the cobble.

Marian gasped in horror when she saw Aleta fall from the edge of town, and she saw the blood pool on the road.

Priestess Trinna screamed when she saw Aleta fall from near the graveyard, and she saw the blood pool on the road.

Jemima saw Aleta fall from behind Marian, having slipped through the same back alleys she had to catch up with her, and pulled Marian away, but never saw the blood pool on the road.

The guards turned and watched Aleta's blood pool on the road.

Aleta's blood pooled on the road, flowing amongst the cracks and gaps in the cobblestones, slowly forming a thick line towards the graveyard, like a dark red snail's trail.

## Chapter Ten: The Night is Long, Part One

Quilla tilted herself towards the Golden Arrow, letting momentum do most of the work. Her right arm was holding her coat in place on her back, red blood staining the green fabric to make an unseemly and unsightly brown, while she clung to the axe with her left hand.

The last thing she heard was a scream from far away, and she could hear no footsteps behind her. The question kept running through her head as she ran through the forest, crashing through the rusted gate and almost breaking it off its hinges, skidding down the slope, and barging through the door to the tavern. Everybody turned to face her. She hobbled in, panting and sweating, placed the axe gently and carefully on a table near the entrance, took a step forward while everybody stepped back, and fell face-first to the floor.

Deryn stood from a chair near the bar and stomped over, shouting for help in the language Marian wasn't here to not understand.

Marian wasn't there to hear it because Marian was being dragged by Jemima back to her house. Jemima picked the lock on the back door and opened it with her shoulder, then let go of Marian's arm and ran upstairs to check on the axe before running back down to an exasperated and traumatised Marian.

"You got it? The crown?" she asked.

"I... Is that... What?" Marian gasped.

"The crown! The Prince's crown! You got it?"

"Jemima... Aleta's dead."

Outside, the guards stood over Aleta's body. The guard on the right had dragged himself from the pond and hobbled over, soaked through again after changing his clothes earlier. Priestess Trinna had also run over.

"What do we do?" asked the guard on the left.

"I... I didn't mean to knock into her. I'm..." Said the guard from the back entrance who knocked her over.

Priestess Trinna managed to keep a level head, having forced most of her emotions out through her scream.

"Go. All four of you, go. Doubtless other guards heard the scream. You four go and catch the man with the axe... I will give blessings to this woman."

The guards looked at each other, hesitating. The guard from the back entrance who didn't knock Aleta over breathed in sharply and spoke.

"We're not supposed to take orders from you, our orders come from..."

"The Chief of the Guard?" Trinna questioned, "Who will come here and ask who did this?"

The guards looked at each other again with wide eyes like animals caught in front of predators, and they nodded, and they ran into the forest in search of Quilla.

All was silent for a moment.

"You can get up now," Priestess Trinna stated calmly, "I've seen enough dead bodies to know when somebody's faking."

All was silent for another moment, before Aleta gasped for air and rolled onto her back, then up into a sitting position. She reached up and pulled an empty blood bag from underneath her hair.

"Do you want to know what's going to happen?" Aleta asked.

Priestess Trinna said nothing.

"You will tell the guards I stood up and walked away, but you will give them my description incorrectly. Tell them I am Mediterranean, yes. But tell them I am young, with red hair. Tell nobody where I go." Aleta said.

"Another secret," Trinna mumbled to herself, "Another secret to keep..."

"Tell. Nobody. Where I go." Aleta repeated.

"Yes. Okay."

"And promise me you will keep the girls safe."

"Yes."

"Promise."

"Promise."

"Good. Goodbye."

Aleta stood, wiping fake blood from her face, and skulked into the back alley leading to Marian's house.

"*Dead?*" Jemima gulped, "DEAD? She was okay, she was running towards the forest…"

"A guard knocked her over," Marian explained, trying to hold back tears, "And the blood… Oh, Jemima, the blood…"

Jemima stepped forward and pulled Marian into a hug.

"There was nothing you could have done." She said.

"If I'd planned differently it wouldn't have happened," Marian said, sniffing, "If I'd suggested things that were just slightly different she'd still be alive…"

"It wasn't your fault, Marian." Assured Jemima.

"You're right. It wasn't." came a voice from behind.

They gasped. Marian turned, and Jemima let go. They stood next to each other, instinctively reaching for daggers in their pockets, before realising who it was.

Aleta stood before them, green coat caked in fake blood.

"I'm alive, girls. Entirely alive, and well. Here is what is going to happen. You will take the crown to the tavern tomorrow morning, and you will tell the people there that I am dead, but reveal to Paloma- and Paloma only- that I am alive, and well. She will ask you a question, and you will respond: the beach. Goodbye, girls. Goodnight. Cheer up. Kiss."

Aleta stepped backwards through the door, closed it, and disappeared into the night.

There was silence in the hallway, as Marian and Jemima were entirely taken aback.

There was silence in the road, as Priestess Trinna waited for more guards.

There was silence in the tavern as Xiang handed Paloma stitching to mend Quilla's wound, and as Celinda held the door open so everybody, including the bard, could leave.

"So she isn't dead." Jemima said, clarifying to herself more than Marian.

"No. Yes. No. Yes, she isn't dead. No, she's not dead." Marian stammered.

"And we got the crown."

"Yes. Yes, I have that. It's here."

Marian pulled the crown from her pocket. It really was like an ugly hat. Unlike most crowns, it was wide-brimmed, most likely in case any of the needlessly large jewels fell off. It was definitely the crown of an unappreciated Prince, or simply one with awful taste.

For the first time since leaving the tower, Marian smiled.

"I thought... I was honestly heartbroken," she said, "I couldn't bear to see her lying there, but... She's... And you're... "

"There's no need to say it all," Jemima smiled too, "Just put the crown down."

Marian dropped the crown without hesitation. Jemima took her hand and squeezed it gently, reassuringly, even perhaps lovingly.

And they kissed. Their lips were as warm as their mutually flushed faces, and Marian's hands were on Jemima's hips, and Jemima's hands were in Marian's hair. They kissed, and it felt right.

Jemima began to take off Marian's coat, unbuttoning it at the front, and throwing it off Marian's shoulders, letting it fall to the floor. Marian felt exposed, and slightly pulled away from the kiss, giving enough time for Jemima to whisper a quiet command.

"Take mine off too, you silly thing." She said.

Marian kissed back, hard, and threw Jemima's coat to the ground. Jemima pushed Marian against the wall, and they kissed more, their breaths sharper and louder and more frequent now.

Quite suddenly, Marian pushed Jemima away.

"Just… Just wait." She said, gasping for air.

"You don't want…? Is it… Is it because we've not known each other long? Or are you not… This way inclined? Oh no. I'm sorry, I thought…" Jemima said, feeling embarrassed for initiating anything now.

"No… Yes. I. I want to carry on. But there's something you should know, before… Anything."

"… Go on?"

"I wasn't always… Called Marian."

"… If you're worried about me calling out the wrong name…"

"It's not that. I mean… Marian's a girl's name."

"Yes…"

"But I didn't always have a girl's name."

"Your parents must've had a sense of humour then?"

"Not exactly... My parents... Thought they had a boy."

Comprehension dawned on Jemima's face.

"Oh! Oh. Oh? You're. You're...?"

"Yes. Transgender."

There was silence for the briefest moment.

"Okay!" Jemima said, smiling and moving forward to kiss Marian again.

"Wait, wait, wait, wait," Marian interrupted, "You know what that means, don't you?"

"Yes, of course!"

"Then what does it mean?" Marian asked, folding her arms, not letting Jemima closer.

"It means... You're a woman? It means you're a woman. It means that for a little while people thought you weren't but then it turned out you were."

Marian gestured with her hand for Jemima to carry on.

"I don't know what you want me to say."

"Do you honestly not care?"

"About what?"

"About what it means. That it means I might have... Not quite the same things you have. Up top, everything's... As you'd expect. But maybe not below."

"Oh."

There was a pause.

"Listen, Marian. I don't know about you, but I'm as gay as the night is long, we're both women and what I want most in my life right now is for us to take off the rest of our clothes and make the most of the fact that the night is as long as I am gay."

Marian unfolded her arms, and Jemima kissed her again, softly this time.

"Do you want to do that?" Jemima asked, lips curling into a quiet smile.

"Yes." Marian replied.

# Intermission

And so they did.

They kissed again, and Jemima moved her hands down Marian's back, and placed her palms delicately on Marian's rear, and then hugged it with her fingers, making Marian gasp into her mouth.

They kissed harder, and Marian ran her hands through Jemima's hair, not quite able to believe what was happening, but having little time to try to comprehend it before Jemima picked her up. She hadn't been expecting her to be able to do that.

Jemima carried Marian into the front room of the house, and almost threw her onto the couch, before climbing on top of her, straddling her.

She felt a lump beneath her, and she was overcome with an urge to lean over and bite Marian's neck.

Marian felt Jemima's teeth sink into her neck, and she moaned, involuntarily, and a little louder than she'd ever thought she would. She twitched beneath Jemima, pushing her lower half closer into her, and then moved her hands from Jemima's hair to the front of her shirt.

Jemima felt the lump beneath her push against her even more, and her face grew hot. Before she knew it, Marian's hands were on her chest, her fingers slipping through gaps between the buttons of her shirt.

Marian tore open Jemima's shirt, revealing functional but fancy underwear, and then quickly slipped her hands behind Jemima's back, unclasping the underwear and letting it hang down.

Jemima grabbed Marian's wrists, and pushed them down to the couch, and then let go.

Marian immediately moved her hands back up to Jemima's chest.

Jemima grabbed Marian's wrists again, and placed them kindly but firmly back on the couch. Marian, getting the message, kept them there as Jemima leaned back.

She slipped off her open shirt by the shoulders, one at a time. First the left, taking special care to move it excruciatingly slowly down her arm, and then the right, doing the same. She dropped the shirt idly to the floor, as if it was of no consequence that she was now practically sat on top of Marian almost half naked.

Then, she let the already loose underwear fall off completely, and her chest was bare, and Marian took in every detail. She noticed how Jemima's left breast was slightly smaller than the right, and she noticed stretch marks like lines of lightning on her hips, and she noticed a small, single freckle just below her ribs. She wanted to kiss it, but it would be an impossible movement. For now, she noted its position, and decided privately that she would kiss the freckle another time. Perhaps in the morning.

She motioned to sit upwards, to kiss Jemima's lips in lieu of a freckle and to touch her in as many places as possible, but Jemima once more pinned down Marian's arms, and then leaned in, let her lips lightly caress Marian's neck, and then moved up slightly higher so that her mouth was barely centimetres away from Marian's ear.

"*Take yours off too, you silly thing.*" She whispered.

Marian lifted slightly, reaching behind her own back, unclasping her tunic.

Jemima raised off Marian for a moment, resting on her knees which were placed resolutely on either side of Marian's legs, and untied the belt around Marian's waist. The tunic, all Marian had been wearing, was loose now, and she had just enough room to slide out of it, pulling it upwards over her head.

Marian was not wearing a bra. Her breasts were larger than Jemima's, and she had more freckles, and a tiny bruise below her collarbone.

Jemima glanced down, and saw the bulge that had previously been pushing against her. It seemed desperate to be free of Marian's lower underwear.

The word transgender pushed itself to the forefront of both of their minds. For Marian, it represented both gain and loss simultaneously- gaining understanding of who she was, fully, without question, but losing people close to her in the process of explaining it. For Jemima, it was a piece of trivia she had just learned about a girl she'd very recently met. With no idea of the history behind the word, to Jemima it was just an explanation for Marian's body being slightly different to her own.

The word lingered for a moment like a cloud hovering over a park, never quite raining, though its very presence threatened a storm.

Marian sat up, and they kissed more, softly, and slowly, for a moment.

Then their chests pushed together, and they lost control, and the cloud was blown eastward and forgotten.

They were a mess, grabbing and scratching and kissing and biting and gasping and moaning and pulling each other's hair, and in the midst of all of it, Jemima moved her hand down Marian's stomach, and touched her above her lower underwear.

Marian recoiled at the contact, and Jemima whipped her hand away. Marian looked down at herself, and back up at Jemima, and they locked eyes.

"Do you want...?" Jemima whispered.

"Yes," Marian smiled as she leaned in closer to Jemima, who slowly reached for the hem of Marian's underwear, which she teased a finger under, and then pulled down, letting Marian's most personal secret out into the open, "Yes."

## Chapter Eleven: The Night is Long, Part Two

"Yes," Paloma said, applying bandages to Quilla's back, "You're going to be fine."

Quilla had woken up during the stitching, screaming in pain and struggling to hold back tears as she kicked her legs in agony, unable to move anywhere else.

"It is but a flesh wound," Paloma continued, finishing the bandages, "But it's delicate, and it will sting. I wouldn't advise heavy lifting. Speaking of which…"

She leaned back, and turned her head upwards to face Deryn, who was leaning against a wall.

"Could you get the axe?"

Deryn didn't respond, or move. Celinda sighed from a chair near the doorway.

"Cuddio y fwyell…" Celinda said to Deryn. Deryn nodded, picked up the axe, and walked into the back room. Paloma turned back to Quilla.

"I know you don't want to be answering questions right now, but this one's important," she said, assertively but not angry, "Did you see my mother, when you were running?"

Quilla thought, and breathed, and got her words in order.

"No, I didn't. I'm sorry, Pal. I think she might have been arrested," and abruptly turning to anger, "Because that fucking Marian didn't think her plan through."

Celinda raised a hand. "Now, that is not…"

Quilla turned onto her stomach and sat up.

"It absolutely is."

"You don't know what I'm going to say."

"I do. You're going to tell me it's not fair, and that I shouldn't blame her without knowing what's happening out there."

"… It turns out you do know what I was going to say, dear, yes. Well done."

"Yes. Exactly. So don't patronise me. It was Marian's fault. If she hadn't stole the axe in the first place, I wouldn't have been there, and…"

"*And*," Celinda interrupted, "Have you forgotten *why* she stole the axe, young lady?"

There was silence. The past few days had been filled with silences, pockmarking conversations like snails on a white wall.

"She stole it to do something *good*. She stole it because she wanted to save a life, Quilla. That is *precisely what we stand for* as members of the Hooded Council."

Quilla looked down at her hands.

"And have you also forgotten *why* you were there at all? Do you remember why you were at Marian's house?"

"Please don't…" Quilla muttered.

"Of course I won't. I don't need to say something you already know, do I, *hm*?"

"No, Celinda."

"*No, Celinda.*"

"I'm sorry."

Celinda looked Quilla over, who was still looking at her palms. Xiang entered while this awkward exchange was happening.

"Yes. You are sorry." Celinda finished.

Xiang tried to make the situation less awkward.

"Okay, friends, ladies… I've been for a little walk outside in the woods, and the guards aren't coming this way…" She said, overly cheerily, "In fact they seemed to give up at the old gate, so, that's… Nice, isn't it?"

There was even more silence.

"Okay… Well then. Celinda. How about I go up to the town and have a look around for Aleta?"

Poloma's head jerked up.

"Can I come with you?"

"No," said Celinda, "No you can't go with her. You need to stay and ensure Quilla's wounds aren't infected. Xiang- go alone, dear. Thank you."

Xiang smiled, gave the most inappropriately timed thumbs up sign that has ever been given, and awkwardly shuffled out of the room. Paloma frowned and looked down at Quilla's back. Quilla remained frowning at the floor. Celinda looked at nothing in particular, but frowned nonetheless. Deryn walked back in, and sensed an awkward situation.

"Dydw i ddim gofal…" she mumbled to herself and left the room again.

A while later, more guards finally arrived, finding Trinna leaning wearily against a wall. She spun a lie to them about how the woman on the floor had been okay, and that the blood had been from the assailant's back. They asked for a description of the woman so that they could interview her as a witness, and Trinna told the lie Aleta had requested.

On the other side of the wall, Xiang listened, confused, unable to interrupt without giving herself away.

In Priestess Trinna's house, Patton Cross waited, sometimes looking out of the window but not seeing anything in the darkness of the night, unable to sleep properly having drank seven cups of tea since Trinna left. On her request, he hadn't left the house, to stay safe.

In Marian's house, they made the most of the night.

## Chapter Twelve: The Gaudy Crown

The King's brother woke up, and immediately called for a servant. One rushed into his room, eager to serve, or at least required to.

He looked the servant over from his bed as he threw his blanket off himself, making no efforts to keep the bed presentable. He took a swig of water that had been sitting on his dresser all night, and did not notice, in his sleepy haze, the lack of any sort of crown to be seen.

"Where the fuck is your uniform?" the Prince asked, after rubbing his eyes with his palms.

"It has been misplaced in the night, sir," the servant explained, "I am sorry for appearing unprofessional. Is there anything I can do to make it up to you, sir?"

"No," he said, "You're fired. Shit off."

The servant nodded and left with a slight whimper just loud enough for the Prince to hear and smile to himself.

He carried on with his morning. He walked out of his room, barefoot, in his nightgown, and stood at the window, hands on his hips.

"What can you all see?" he called out to the servants stood behind him.

"A sunny day?" One of them asked, scared of meeting the same fate as his previous co-worker.

"A SUNNY FUCKING DAY," bellowed the Prince, "Now fetch me my slippers. It's *breakfast time*."

A servant ran to his room and fetched his slippers for him. He sat in one of the chairs by the shelves of books and put his feet up on the table. The servant, with an unseen grimace, slid the slippers on the Prince's unwashed feet.

"Now," the Prince said, "What are we having?"

"The cook should be here any moment, sir, with your usual."

"Oh fuck," The Prince gasped, taking his feet off the table, "Oh absolutely shitting fuck that sounds good. Do you know the night I've had? Bad dreams all around. Kept thinking I heard screaming, and other such irritating noises. Have a look into that. Maybe consider making me deaf, so I don't have to bother with noises at all. Maybe consider burning the weird fucking mermaid portrait in that room. If I'm staying here, I'm staying here in a room I'm fucking comfortable in, yes? Yes. Burn the painting."

"My lord," gasped the servant, "That painting is a priceless antique painted by none other than the great Melissa B…"

"BURN IT," shouted the Prince, making the servant jump back in surprise, "FUCKING BURN IT, IT'LL BE FUNNY."

The rest of the servants all turned to face the servant at the table.

"Yes, your lordship."

"Ship?"

"Lordship, sir."

"Burn the other one."

"I'm sorry, sir?"

"BURN THE OTHER ONE. THE OTHER PAINTING. IT'S A SHIPWRECK. FUCKING WRECK IT."

The cook entered, holding a large platter of assorted meats.

"Oh this is a good day," he said as the cook placed his meal down, "Do you know, I'd rather like to wear my crown. Could you go and fetch it?"

It was a good morning for the Prince.

The servant dashed into the Prince's bedroom and looked for the crown. The servant could not see the crown. The servant reluctantly moved the blanket which hung off the edge of the bed, to see if the crown had fallen under there. The servant did not find the crown, and could not tell if the bed was cold or damp. The servant sincerely hoped the bed was cold, as a damp bed has no redeeming qualities.

The servant had to break the news, and the silence.

"My lord," the servant said, pulling confidence from a hidden reserve nobody had anticipated, "Your crown has been misplaced in the night."

Elsewhere, a good morning was in progress. As sunlight pierced through the blinds, Marian awoke on her bed that was mostly a pile of pillows, and for the first time in her life she was waking up next to somebody else. Jemima was sleeping, lying flat on her back, and Marian kissed her on the cheek.

Jemima woke up, smiling at the contact, and stretched out her back. She opened her eyes, but immediately shut them again to shield them from the sunlight. She curled towards Marian.

"Is it really morning?" she asked.

"It is," Marian replied, twirling her hands through Jemima's hair, "Which means, unfortunately, we have things to do."

"Let's just pretend we don't for a while…" Jemima moaned, nestling further into Marian's neck.

"Jemima." Marian stated.

"No…" Jemima replied, cuddling closer, "Don't say I have to get up…"

"I will say that, because we have to. Not saying it doesn't make it less true."

Jemima put on a dramatic display of rolling out of bed, stretching her limbs wildly in all directions, and eventually standing up, towering over Marian in a distinct state of undress, the sun shining through the window to present her body like strategically placed lights in an art gallery.

"Well?" Jemima asked, folding her arms, "Why aren't you getting up then?"

"Enjoying the view, mainly."

Jemima grabbed at Marian's arm and pulled her out of bed, and both of them got dressed.

Having neglected to bring a change of clothes, Jemima wore some of Marian's old ones. Specifically, an old white shirt that was far too long on the sleeves, casual leggings, her own boots and a viridian velvet waistcoat Marian wasn't aware she owned that Jemima pulled from somewhere in the depths of the wardrobe. Marian simply pulled on her old dress- the black belted tunic with green floral pattern that she had worn the day she left her family.

She left home holding Jemima's hand, entirely conscious of it this time, carrying her coat under her other arm, the gaudy crown tucked into a pocket.

"YOU'RE FIRED," boomed The Prince as he swung an arm sideways and knocked several forks off the table, "YOU'RE ALL FUCKING FIRED. ALL OF YOU, YOU USELESS TWIGS."

The servants all left, some of them holding back tears, others holding back cheers of joy at no longer being forced to work under this monster, who now sat alone, a plate of unfinished assorted meats in front of him.

He punched it. He punched the plate, and he punched each meat individually, and just to be certain, he punched the table. His crown was missing.

Outside the room were footsteps, and scraping wood, coming closer as they moved up the stairs. The door creaked open worriedly and the Chief of the Guard, Leonard Garden-Hand, approached the Prince. He was an older man, with a well-groomed silver beard, and the lower half of his left calf had been replaced with a thick wooden prosthetic. He stepped over to the Prince- sensible shoe first, then wooden foot, in a continuous rhythm, while the Prince stared down at a broken plate, scattered meats and a bloody hand.

"My crown's gone, Leonard," the King's brother whimpered, "It's gone and I don't have it any more."

Leonard nodded, and sat at the other side of the table.

"I heard. We'll find it," he said in the voice of a parent soothing their child, "We'll find the bastard who took it, I promise."

"It's really ruined my day, you know," whined William, "It was going to be positively wondrous. I was going to get the servants to burn a portrait, but NOW, NOW I DON'T EVEN *HAVE* ANY SERVANTS…"

"It's okay, my lord." Leonard spoke, "It's going to be entirely okay. We will find the one who stole your crown. I'm going out on a limb here, but- two major thefts in two nights?"

The Prince looked up.

"It's probably the same person," Leonard continued, "And I've got a plan to root them out."

Prince William Alan Anchor wiped his wet eyes but only ended up spreading blood and crumbs over his brow.

The forest looked different in the sunlight. It was a brilliant green, and much too warm for snails, but squirrels and other tiny creatures were truly in their element. A few small birds flapped past, feathers fluttering over Marian's hair. They made their way to the tavern in the same way as the previous night, and they arrived without incident.

Jemima opened the front door and peaked in.

"Nobody's here," she said.

"I suppose it's too early?" Marian suggested.

"Yes- yes, it must be. You know I've never actually come here in the day…"

Jemima sat down, and Marian hung her coat on a stand by the door. She lay the crown in front of Jemima.

"Ugh," Jemima groaned, "It's horrible, isn't it?"

Marian nodded, and then began to smile.

"What? What's funny?"

Marian picked up the crown and motioned to put it on Jemima's head.

"NO DO NOT DO THAT DO NOT EVEN THINK ABOUT DOING THAT." Jemima stated in one loud, run-on sentence, not stopping for breath as her chair scraped on the floor and she stumbled backwards, Marian in pursuit.

"You don't want to wear the crown?"

"No! No I don't!"

"But then you'll be a *Lady*."

"I- I don't want to be a *Lady* if it involves wearing *that*..."

Jemima felt a bump behind her. She was cornered, her back against the bar.

"Marian..." she began, watching the crown get closer and closer to her face, "MARIAN..." she continued, the crown now only inches from her, "*MARIAN LAVERNE STOKE YOU PUT THAT HORRENDOUS HAT DOWN RIGHT THIS SECOND.*"

Marian stopped, and lowered the crown, and tried not to laugh, which proved entirely impossible as Jemima began to laugh first.

They laughed for a good minute, before Marian held up a hand.

"When did I tell you my middle name?" She asked, short of breath.

"Last night," Jemima answered, leaning back against the bar, holding both of Marian's hands and pulling her closer, "Shortly before I untied..."

She was interrupted by the sound of somebody clearing their throat. Deryn was stood in the doorway to the room with the round table. Marian and Jemima jumped apart.

"How- how, how long have you been...?" Marian began, but Deryn only stared, "Oh. Oh, right. I'd forgotten."

Deryn rolled her eyes and mumbled something, more words Marian didn't know the meaning of. She walked right past them and out of the front door. Jemima and Marian sat back down at the table, and considered the crown.

"So Aleta's..." Marian began,

"Dead, as far as anybody else is concerned." Jemima concluded.

"But she's actually..."

"Alive, which we are to tell nobody but Paloma."

"And the crown..."

"Means you passed the test, and you're in the Council legitimately."

"And you and I..."

"Are girlfriends now, heavily infatuated, and.... Wait. I. What? That's not part of the recap!"

Marian giggled to herself.

"I just wanted to make sure we were on the same page." She explained, and the front door opened again. Celinda was silhouetted by sunlight.

"Hello, young women." She said, stepping in. She stood in front of the table and picked up the crown. Deryn followed but again walked straight through to the back room.

"Hello, we..." Marian began.

"Yes. Yes, I'm holding it, dear."

"But we have something else to say."

Celinda was busy looking at the jewels on the crown. She touched one, lightly, just with the tip of her finger. It was real. She smiled to herself, and absently replied.

"What… What do you have to say?"

Marian looked over at Jemima, who made brief eye contact and then spoke.

"It's about Aleta. I'm sorry Celinda, there's… No easy way to say this."

Celinda looked down from the crown.

"She's dead, Celinda."

Celinda stared, and gently placed the crown back on the table.

"Dead."

"Yes."

"That wasn't a question."

Silence.

More silence.

A third wave of silence.

"Who killed her?" Celinda asked at last.

Standing, Jemima spoke again. Marian's heart raced.

"She fell, on the cobble road, and she…"

"Who. Killed. Her? Tell me the truth, Jemima."

They met each other's eyes.

"A guard knocked her down."

"Which guard?"

"I don't know. He was a man."

"They're all men. What did he look like?"

"Like a man."

"Are you saying all men look the same?"

"I might be."

"Then the events of last night have done nothing to waver your resolve or change you for the worse. You are stronger than ever, and that is what we need."

Celinda picked up the crown and left, into the room with the round table. There was a fourth silence, before Celinda broke it again.

"Well?" She called from the other room, "Aren't you coming in?"

Marian and Jemima hurried into the back room, where Celinda and Deryn were already sat.

"You two ladies are positively glowing," Celinda said as they sat down, holding eye contact with Marian the whole time, "Which is a reassurance. Your glow is a brightness in a dark time, and infinitely prettier than the sun. Now- a question remains, dears. Does Paloma know?"

"No," Marian stated bluntly, "We were hoping she'd be here."

"Well doubtless she's out looking for her mother..." Celinda trailed off.

The conversation continued, detailing the events of the night. Eventually, Quilla entered, and she cried. Jemima cried because Quilla cried, and because she knew the reasons she shouldn't be. Xiang entered, and did not cry. She sat as stoic as Deryn, across from her at the round table, like two opposing Queens in a game of circular chess.

And then, Paloma. Paloma came in last, after a couple of hours.

"I've been looking for mother all day," she said, "She's nowhere. She's just... Nowhere."

Celinda turned to Marian and Jemima, and gestured with her hand for them to lead her back out of the room. They obliged.

Outside, in the bar room, people had begun to arrive. The bard was sat in the corner, staring at the door as though waiting for somebody. A man stood at the bar polishing a cup. Another man smiled as the three women walked past. They nodded politely and left through the front door, and found a quiet area of the forest.

"What's this about? Why can't you tell me indoors?" Paloma questioned.

"It's… Complicated," Jemima began, "Because it involves a lie."

And they explained. It was difficult, but they explained. There were questions, but they explained.

They went back indoors. Xiang glared at them as they sat down and Paloma faked tears.

In the town, people were still rushing, making the most of the last few minutes before the sun set and, more likely than otherwise, it began to rain. A crier walked out into the swarming square.

"HEAR YE ALL," he chanted, ringing a bell, "ON THE THIRTEENTH OF THE MONTH, THERE WILL BE A CONTEST… FOR WHOSOEVER MAY BE VICTORIOUS OVER THE PRINCE… WILL BE AWARDED A SOLID GOLDEN SWORD… AND ALLOWED TO EXECUTE THE DISGRACED KNIGHT, SIR PATTON CROSS."

The Prince watched from his open window, smiling. A new, fresh servant approached with a glass of wine, but he shooed her away, pointing at the table.

A confused, lost snail poked out of its shell on the ledge of the window.

The Prince crushed it with the side of his fist.

## Chapter Thirteen: Robin Hood

Though she had forgotten now, Marian had heard the name Robin Hood before.

After leaving the house where her family had lived, she found herself at a small inland village named Dove's Rest. It was, by all accounts, the worst village in the country. It had once had a twin town somewhere in mainland Europe, but a few years prior to Marian's arrival an ambassador from this other town had come to visit and died in a tragic and unexplained manner. Everybody's best guess was that he had taken one look at the state of Dove's Rest and decided life simply wasn't worth it any more.

The road was made primarily of holes, and had hardly constituted a road for years. Nobody bothered to repair it because nobody ever came in or out. The buildings were run-down, broken, their paint had faded to an indeterminate colour somewhere between brown and grey, and the walls seemed to be tearing at the seams like the shirt of somebody who refuses to admit to themselves that they have grown too tall to wear their childhood clothing. The air tasted of sour regret and an almost mournful and disturbingly wet bitterness. The whole village had a faint smell of beetroot about it, and nobody knew why, because nobody there even liked beetroot. Nobody there even ate beetroot. Nobody there even remembered what beetroot looked like. Marian was the first visitor in as long as anybody there bothered to keep track of.

She was hungry, and not for beetroot, so she headed to the inn near the centre of town. Her heart raced as she approached the door, concerned about what was on the other side. She wasn't looking forward to the inevitability of everybody turning and glowering at this timid newcomer, as they had in so many towns before. Something about new visitors, she had discovered, often made drunk people angry, as if their presence was somehow infringing on their home, or as if their visit would permanently alter the town in some abstract but clearly problematic way.

As it turned out, she had nothing to worry about. Barely anyone registered her as she walked in, only the innkeeper himself, and probably some of the mould on the walls that had, no doubt, become sentient by now.

She asked for a loaf of bread, and the innkeeper told her to try the baker. They didn't have any left in the inn. She asked if the inn had any free rooms, and he asked what she meant by free, and she asked if the inn had any rooms she could stay in for the night, and he asked why she'd be needing multiple rooms, and she asked if she could just buy a room for the night and he said yes, of course.

She handed over a trickle of coins that dripped into the innkeeper's hand as water dripped from the wall behind him. It wasn't raining outside. Marian had no idea where that dripping was coming from. Having secured the room, she followed his advice, and left to go to the bakery.

On the way, she pickpocketed seven people, who all swayed aimlessly through the streets, emotionless apart from boredom. She felt sort of guilty for pickpocketing them, but that quickly dissipated. She reached the bakery, walked in, took a loaf of bread, and walked out.

That was how simple it was to steal a loaf of bread in Dove's Rest, which she was beginning to suspect was a name chosen long ago, before the odour of impossible beetroot permeated every surface.

All she wanted now was a drink of water, and to eat her bread in peace, so she went back to the inn, and asked which room was hers. The innkeeper said none of the rooms were hers, and she said she'd bought one for the night, and he said she hadn't, and she said she had, and he said he had no rooms free, and she said that's because he sold the last one to her, and he said actually yes that sounds right, and she asked for a flagon of water, and he said that seems doable.

She sat on her bed, and regretted it. She wasn't sure if it was cold or damp. She sincerely hoped it was the former. She could tolerate a cold bed if she wrapped herself tightly enough, but a damp bed had precisely zero redeeming qualities. Either way, it was bumpy. It was the worst bed she had ever sat on. It was probably, she thought, the worst bed in the world.

As she ate the bread, and drank the water, she thought of all she had left behind, and she did not miss it. She did not miss her family, she did not miss her friends. She did not miss her house, or her street, or her town. All she allowed herself to briefly miss was air that did not smell of beetroot, and her bed, but even this did not last long as her thoughts were interrupted by the sound of the inn door swinging open. She listened as three guards entered.

"Do you think it was Robin Hood, then?" one of them asked.

"Yeah," said the second, "Definitely, like."

"Who's that then?" asked the third.

"You *don't know*?" the first probed incredulously.

"No…" the third admitted.

"He's a right bastard, is Robin Hood," said the Innkeeper, "He's been in here overnight, as well. I had a diamond ring, back in the day. My old man gave it to me, it was his wedding ring, wasn't it? But then, next thing I know, Robin Hood's rolled into town and my ring's fucked off to who knows where."

"He's a thief then?" the third guard asked.

"He's more than just a thief," clarified the second guard, "He's THE thief."

"What's he robbed this time then?" the Innkeeper asked.

They mentioned something about a book, and Marian lost interest as the conversation turned to talk of humdrum life in Dove's Rest, and she tried to get as much rest herself as was possible on this bed that was so full of lumps that she thought the mattress had been stuffed with beetroots.

In the morning, she awoke before anybody else in the whole village had managed to drag up enough motivation from the core of their being to force themselves out of bed, stole back the money she'd bought the room for, picked the lock on the bakery and took some more bread for good measure and then travelled on to nicer places, forgetting she'd ever visited such a disgusting blot on the face of the landscape, and forgetting she'd ever heard the name Robin Hood.

But tonight was the night. In the tavern which smelled of honey wine and bitter ale- which were much nicer smells than beetroot now she had become accustomed to them- she would meet THE thief. She would meet Robin Hood. All were sat at the round table now, except of course for Aleta. They all mourned her passing, though three of them were lying and one of them was enormously and interminably suspicious. Two of them did not speak, one by choice and the other by unknowable reasoning.

"For what it's worth," confessed Quilla, "I'm sorry I doubted you."

Marian smiled, and Jemima smiled too, squeezing her hand in reassurance under the table.

"It was reasonable doubt," Marian said, looking down at the table, "I suppose it can be difficult to believe that somebody would steal something so dangerous."

"Oh! Oh, Paloma, do you remember…" Jemima began.

"I know exactly what you're going to say," Paloma replied, "You're going to ask me if I remember the night mother stole the cane."

"The cane?" Marian asked.

"Oh, Paloma, Marian hasn't heard the story! You *have* to tell it."

Celinda raised a hand. "It is up to Paloma… She may not wish to talk about her mother at the moment, hm?"

Paloma sighed, and looked down, putting on quite the act.

"I think I'd like to tell the story. I think it's important for tonight to be… Exactly the night we'd have expected otherwise."

Celinda nodded, and smiled silently, and whispered something to Deryn. Paloma began the story.

"There was a Duchess, you see. She was so pale, and so large, and she wore so much jewellery that from a distance she looked herself like a walking pearl."

There was a chorus of mild laughter around the table.

"It would have been easy to take the jewellery, of course. We've all stolen necklaces. I've got a whole drawer full of them. But the real prize was her cane, the one she always walked with."

Marian turned to Jemima, who was enraptured in the story. A twinge of jealousy shot through Marian, establishing itself as a deep red glow and settling in her cheeks. She edged slightly closer to Jemima, who once more squeezed her hand, turning and smiling as Paloma continued her story.

"It was made of thick, dark oak, and the handle was carved to be the shape of a duck's head, and in its beak… A solid, flawless ruby."

Marian's eyes widened, and she leaned closer.

"Mother waited until the Duchess was sitting alone in a restaurant, her attendants having gone to fetch her a drink. The cane was leaning against the table, and, posing as a waiter, she took it, and left the restaurant."

Jemima smiled broadly.

"But that wasn't even the end of it. She changed out of the waiter's clothes outside, hid the cane behind the building, and then ran back in…"

"This is the best bit." Jemima whispered to Marian.

"And she shouted for the whole restaurant to hear that ROBIN HOOD JUST RAN THIS WAY, AND HE WAS HOLDING A CANE!"

All at the table burst into laughter. Xiang's wary expression even turned momentarily into a smile. Marian wasn't sure she understood- it sounded like a tale of victory, but she felt like she was missing a joke.

"I'm sorry to ask again, but- will I get to meet Robin Hood now? Now I've passed the test."

Everybody at the table turned to each other in a moment of sudden realisation.

"That is a very good question to ask, dear." Celinda beamed.

"Robin Hood's here right now, in fact." Quilla smirked.

"Really?" Marian asked, "And can I meet him?"

"Yes- Yes, I imagine you could. There are no problems with that, are there ladies?" Celinda asked the table. Everybody shook their head. Deryn shook her head too, which Marian found irritating.

Can she understand what we're saying? Can she? Did she laugh at the story? I can't remember. I can't ask her because she doesn't respond. I'll just ask Jemima, Marian thought. This sequence of suppositions was then severed by the rest of the women at the table standing, Jemima pulling up Marian by her hand, before letting go.

They pushed Marian out the door, into the tavern room. People in the bar turned, momentarily confused why all seven of the women were leaving at once, but then a couple of people seemed to understand, and after a few seconds, an excited but muffled buzz filled the air like a chorus of rodents chattering happily.

Then they turned her to a door she hadn't yet walked through or even seen opened, next to the bar. Jemima stepped forward and unlocked it, and they made Marian walk through first.

There were shelves of gold. There were shelves of jewels. There were shelves of everything one would want to steal. It was as though a miniature dragon had taken roost in the building and hoarded as many trinkets as possible, and everything glimmered and shined in the light of a lamp Quilla carried in, and hung on a hook by the door.

Celinda moved past Marian, and placed the gaudy crown on a high shelf. Leaning against a low shelf beneath it was a thick, dark oak cane ornamented with a duck's head holding a ruby in its beak.

Deryn moved past Marian, and placed the headsman's axe gently down on the floor. Even the floor was covered in ornaments- vases, small piles of plates, decorative jugs, and patterned tankards all flourished in miniature communities and neat rows, and it was beautiful.

Xiang closed the door behind them all, and Marian was very aware of her palms beginning to sweat, and her sudden urge to bite her own bottom lip.

"Is it... Bad... That I want to steal *all of this*?" She asked between stunted breaths.

Everybody smiled, and Jemima tittered.

"So… When… I mean, where… Will Robin Hood meet me here?"

The women turned to each other, not answering, waiting for Marian to realise her error.

"I mean… Where is he?"

Celinda finally spoke.

"My dear, you do a disservice to yourself to call yourself by "*he*"."

Marian broke her gaze from the stacks of striking luxuries, and furrowed her brow as she looked over at Celinda, who simply raised her arms and gestured to the other end of the room.

On the far wall, there was a mirror. It was ornately decorated, and the largest mirror Marian had ever seen.

The mirror, naturally, showed her reflection.

She was stood in the middle, surrounded by women in green. Celinda stood on her left, arms outstretched towards the mirror. Deryn stood on her right, leaning casually against a shelf. Behind her to the right were Xiang and Quilla, both of whom gave mostly unexpected smiles, and behind her to the left was Jemima, who stood forward ever so slightly and slipped her hand into Marian's.

"I'm…?" Marian gasped.

"Not just you," Jemima spoke softly, "All of us."

Marian turned to Jemima, whose eyes glistened with welling water in the lamp light, and Jemima continued.

"Do you see? The legend of Robin Hood… It's a lie. It's a lie we made. Wherever we go, we tell people of a man named Robin who steals from the rich and gives to the poor, who steals for good, who steals for the people who deserve to live. We plant the seeds, and wait for trees to grow, and hide in the forest that results. If people are looking for *one man*… They're not going to consider seven women, are they?" Jemima smiled brightly and broadly, and Marian looked back to the mirror.

"We're more than just thieves, you see." Said Quilla.

"And we're more than just the Hooded Council." Said Xiang.

"We are, in the night, more than just ladies." Said Celinda.

"We are more together than the rest of the world alone." Said Paloma.

"We are more than anybody could ever dream of." Said Jemima.

"Rydym Robin Hood." Said Deryn.

And for the first time Marian understood what she meant. Her grip tightened on Jemima's hand as she saw herself in the mirror and knew exactly who she was, and who they were.

They were together, as Robins in the Night.

# Chapter Fourteen: Matching Coats

Earlier that day, there had been a string of minor thefts.

A young woman walked from a baker to a butcher, and on the way, her pastries went missing.

An old man stepped outside of a pub, and before he knew it, his pockets were empty.

A middle-aged person without a knowable gender sat on a bench at the docks and their bag was stolen from underneath them without them noticing for hours.

This pattern was repeated all over town, and the guards were baffled. By the time they arrived at the scene of one crime, another crime had been committed on the other side of the city altogether, and whenever they sought the advice of Chief Leonard Garden-Hand they were waved away by their colleagues at the tower entrance. Eventually, two of the guards just gave up trying.

When they arrived at the docks to investigate the genderless individual's bag theft, they just sat on the bench themselves and tried to come up with a plan to set the day in order. The one on the right took off his coat and laid it out next to him, and a couple of minutes later the one on the left looked over and noticed it was gone. The one on the right threw a pebble in the water out of anger, but it did not help.

Patton Cross prowled through the back alleys near the cobble road through to the edge of town, a large bag on his back full of useless, insignificant items. He waited until they heard a group of people walk by, and then stepped out of the alleyway, letting the people take in his full description, and letting the rumours circulate of a large, broad, old black man with a shaved head roaming through town with a suspiciously large bag and a guard's coat.

The night prior, Patton had waited for what might have been hours for Priestess Trinna to return, and when she finally did, she told him everything, every detail as she understood it, and Patton made a decision. Sir Patton Cross intended to clear Quilla's name.

But he was not, of course, alone. Shortly after Trinna explained to Patton all that had been happening, Aleta had arrived, clean now, free of fake blood, and they had formulated this plan together.

They would spend the day committing crimes.

The guards, obviously, in their infinite wisdom, had assumed Quilla to be a man the previous night, because of her frame and her shaved head, and the fact that they did not see her face. They had spread the word amongst other guards about this tall, black, dangerous and armed thief, and when the rumours of Patton Cross actively stealing things met their ears, they began to put two and two together and make something vaguely in the shape of what they were led to believe was four.

"Do you think...?" Asked the guard on the right.

"That Patton Cross stole the axe?" Asked the guard on the left.

"It makes sense... Why didn't we think of it sooner?"

"I don't know. Does it make sense?"

"I think so. He must have hidden the axe himself so it couldn't be used against him."

"Fuck. That does make sense."

"I know."

"But how could we arrest him? Every time we get close, he's suddenly on the other side of town!"

These impossibly located crimes had been committed, unbeknownst to the guards, by Aleta, specifically to throw them off, and to distract them for as long as possible.

"And if we do arrest him, what then? We can't execute him! He's hidden the bloody axe!"

The guards slumped back onto the bench in frustration.

"D'you ever just want to quit?" Asked the guard on the right.

"Quit?" Asked the guard on the left.

"As in, stop doing this, like. Guarding. Investigating."

"What else would we do?"

They looked out over the water. The tide was high, and from here they could see for miles, all the way to the horizon.

"We could sail." Stated the guard on the right.

There was a pause filled with the sounds of lazily lapping water.

"We could sail…" The guard on the left repeated.

Shovel in, dirt out, pile it up next to the gravestone, repeat as necessary. It was tricky, though, especially with no practice. Open an old grave, bury the meaningless stolen goods, and leave. Not easy.

Patton and Aleta had never done this before. The dock road was quiet at this time of day, but that wouldn't last long. Aleta was used to avoiding detection, but not in this precise context.

They had finally dug far enough to hide the bag, Aleta shoving it in haphazardly, and Patton immediately covering the hole back up again. They shook hands, and left the graveyard, Aleta heading more towards the city, and Patton turning to the edge of town to follow Aleta's directions.

Priestess Trinna watched nervously from afar, behind her window, as Patton made to leave. She rightfully feared for his safety, and had tried to persuade both Aleta and Patton not to go ahead with this day of crime, but to no avail. They were determined to do good things, and ultimately Trinna could not argue with that.

As Aleta made for back alleys, Patton made for the forest, and Trinna made tea, all of them heard as the town crier made his announcement.

All of their stomachs collectively dropped, and the sun thought that was a good idea and decided to drop too, making a noticeable descent below the horizon.

That evening, just after sunset, Celinda gave Marian a coat. The coat had been made for her in the same style and colour as the coats everybody else wore, in that specific shade of deep green that looked as though it had secrets woven into the fabric, and it had the most convenient array of pockets Marian had ever encountered.

Marian was very enthusiastic about pockets. Her favourite dress had pockets, deep ones, with plenty of space. They were half of the reason she had been attracted to the dress to begin with. And of course, she had added the pockets to her grey tunic herself, to make it easier to carry as much as possible back from graveyards.

There had been one night when she stole a jacket that looked absolutely perfect, but which turned out to have false pockets. It was rare that a thief could feel cheated, as though something she deserved had been taken from her, but a lack of pockets was too much. She brought it back. It wasn't worth stealing.

So now, she was presented with this coat, and it was everything she had ever dreamed of. The one she had brought with her hung forgotten on the stand in the tavern as she and Jemima stood in the mirror room.

"We match." Jemima stated, not harshly, but directly. Nothing else needed to be said, and Marian knew she did not have to reply. They just carried on looking in the mirror at themselves, bordered by shelves of jewels and precious objects that seemed to stretch even further in the reflection, for a private eternity. As the noise in the tavern rose higher in direct combat with the budding smell of roast potatoes, they clung to each other's hands, not daring to comprehend any reason for them to stop.

They stopped when the door opened behind them, and Xiang strode into the room, wearing her own green coat, closed, fastened up to her neck.

"We match." Xiang stated, in a façade of cheeriness.

"I… Yes, we do." Marian replied.

"Lovely! Look at the three of us. Aren't we dashing, friends?"

Jemima cocked her head slightly to the side.

"Is there something wrong, Xiang?" She asked, bluntly, and harshly, "I ask because you've been staring at us with daggers in your eyes all night."

Xiang smiled the fakest smile, and gave the second most inappropriately timed thumbs up that has ever been given.

"Nothing's wrong at all! I'm absolutely fine. A little confused, though…"

Jemima and Marian said nothing.

"Because Quilla left the tavern with Aleta- the *dearly departed, late Aleta-* but her body was nowhere to be found… And even more curiously, the Priestess says a woman with red hair walked away from the scene where Aleta… died."

Jemima and Marian continued saying nothing.

"That's a little weird you see friends because Aleta didn't have red hair, did she?"

Jemima and Marian completed their trilogy of saying absolutely nothing. Their hearts did most of the talking, beating rapidly in heated synchronisation.

"What's going on then, loves?" Xiang asked, smiling an even faker smile than before.

Marian's palm began to sweat all over again, and she missed Jemima's comforting grip. Jemima remained firm, having no visible intention of answering Xiang's question, and none of them said anything, until Marian could not take it anymore, hurling away the burden of muteness that she carried on her shoulders.

"Aleta's alive," she exclaimed, "Entirely alive and well. She's got plans, I think, but she didn't tell us. That's absolutely all we know, but you must *not tell anybody else.*"

A combination of confirmation and incomprehension spread across Xiang's features, and relief washed over Jemima's like a tidal wave finally wearing down a rock.

"You're... Telling me, then, that Aleta faked her death and ran away, and told you to tell us that she'd died, and told Trinna to tell the guards that she was her daughter, but told you to tell her daughter that she was alive, and... Relied on the upsetting nature of the situation distracting us all from the question of where her body was?"

They thought for a moment, and the absurdity of the situation began to settle in all of them. They knew nothing of what Aleta was really planning, and nothing of where she was, and nothing of how she expected her plan to work. They knew what Aleta had told them, and looking at the bigger picture, all of Aleta's explanation had been a few trivial brush strokes over the canvas upon which she was still in the process of crafting a masterpiece of a scheme.

"Yes." Jemima and Marian said in unison.

"I see. Well then." Xiang said.

They remained silent for a moment, and Xiang smiled, a genuine one this time.

"I can't wait to see..."

Patton Cross burst through the door of the tavern.

## Chapter Fifteen: The Golden Sword

A thunderous quietness crashed over the room like the last great roar of a wild beast before the very end. It reverberated around itself, rebounding off walls as Sir Patton Cross, disgraced knight of the King's Guard turned tactical thief, recounted the words of the Town Crier.

Everybody stood and listened to his story. Really, this was the only place he would have been listened to. For a known thief to tell an honest story, he needs to be in the company of people of people who are well acquainted with thieves already.

To begin with, he spoke between small inhalations, having not ran so quickly in longer than he could remember. He was not, in fact, old, though he appeared it. His body was simply aged beyond his years, and he was not in quite the same physical shape he used to be as a younger man.

When he was young, he had lived in a beautiful, thriving village named Dove's Rest. Every day he would run up and down the streets. Every night he would return home to his comfortable family house, sit on his comfortable family couch and eat a comfortable family meal. It was heaven, to Patton. He had not visited there in decades, but he often dreamt of its magnificent odour of freshly cut grass, and he wondered frequently how the village had been getting along without him.

As a child, it had always been his ambition to join the King's Guard, and fight for what he thought was right. What people had told him was right, and what he had believed was right. He was unsatisfied with living in heaven, and craved insatiably to be at the head of a march through hell.

Though a lot of his days and nights were hazy now, he could still remember the day he was finally old enough to join. That day, he packed a simple suitcase with everything he could need: a change of clothes and his birth certificate. As long as he could stay warm, and prove his age and his name, he would be allowed to join, and that is precisely how it worked out. On his nineteenth birthday, he joined the Guard, and fought in the name of the King.

It was currently precisely forty-two years to the day since he joined, but he wasn't aware. He had forgotten the date completely, but a birthday overlooked is a birthday nonetheless, and on his sixty-first birthday he joined the populace of The Golden Arrow, which he rather wished he had known about earlier.

"And finally," he said to the room at large, his lungs having caught up with him, "They say the winner of the contest will... Will be executing me."

There were gasps, and murmurs, and intakes of breath through the nose, and noticeably pointed silences.

"So, and I'm sorry this sounds selfish, but I was wondering if maybe somebody wanted to... Stop that from happening? I understand not many people get one execution halted, and nobody ever gets two, but... I expected to die, and failed to do so. I would like to fail to die again."

Marian stepped forward, pushing through the crowd. Jemima tried, fleetingly, to pull her back, but then thought better of it.

"Did they mention what kind of contest it would be?" she asked plainly and confidently.

She then realised where she was stood- in front of a crowd, in the light of the tavern, with all eyes on her. This was not where she liked to stand. She regretted this decision immediately, but pulled out an old mask of confidence from within herself. She would play the part of somebody assertive in front of many people. She would play Marian Stoke, famous author, creator of the concept of reverse werewolves.

"No." Patton replied. He was not sure he had ever been introduced to Marian Stoke, but something told him this was the woman who had saved him from execution.

"Regardless... Your execution will be stopped. The sword will be mine." Marian stated, putting one arm on her hip, then thinking she probably looked silly and letting it drop again. Nobody seemed to notice this indecision, as they were too busy being shocked. Jemima forced her way to Marian's side.

"You intend to win the sword?" Came Celinda's voice from behind, and everybody turned.

"Yes. I will win the sword." Said Marian Stoke, writer of a series of Five Poems about Dresses and a particularly excellent individual piece under the working title "A Snail's Point of View".

"Hm? You will, will you?"

"I will."

"You're certain?"

"I will win the sword."

There was an uncomfortable lack of noise for longer than could possibly have been necessary.

"Yes. That is the truth. You will." Celinda nodded, and left, walking into the room with the round table.

Marian Stoke, acclaimed author of the classic children's book "Little John's Big Day", turned back to Patton Cross, author of nothing.

"You may sleep easy tonight, my friend," She said, wondering where in the world those words had come from because they were certainly not her own, "For you are under the protection of Marian Hood. Stoke. Marian Stoke. Marian... Marian Hood-Stoke. Author. I wrote a book. It's called "The Backwards Pack". Have you read it?"

Everybody slowly shook their heads. Jemima mouthed "What are you talking about?" while Marian attempted to avoid her eye.

"Thank you... Marian Stoke." Responded Patton, and the room began to buzz with the general chatter of poor life once more. Before Marian could sit Patton down to talk to him personally, Jemima dragged her outside.

"What are you doing? What are you *thinking* what are you *doing* why are you *suddenly an author?*" She asked rapidly, barely a pause between words, her mouth moving like the wings of a hummingbird.

Marian took Jemima's hands in hers.

"I've got to do this, Jemima. I put myself on the path of stealing the axe, and now… Now it's practically my duty. Isn't that the principle of Robin Hood?"

"The point is to steal," Jemima almost whispered, "Not to… Not to compete in something you might *die* in!"

Marian gave a shy but teasing smile, and Jemima blinked wet eyes.

"Never once did I say I was going to compete."

Realisation splashed onto Jemima's face at the same time as a tear which she promptly wiped away.

"I'm going to…" Began Marian.

"… Steal the sword." Finished Jemima.

"Yes."

"That doesn't explain the author situation."

"That's a character I play. It helps me, when I have to speak publicly."

"Do you play a character when you speak to me?"

"No, when I'm with you I'm more myself than anyone."

"We've known each other two nights."

"Yes, and you already know…"

"Your middle name?"

"Close enough."

"Kiss me."

"Please."

"You want *me* to say *please*?"

"I'm not sure."

"Then why did you say it?"

"It was a heated moment."

"It's still a heated moment."

"Are we going to kiss?"

"When *you* say please."

"*Please*."

"That's more like it."

They kissed against the wall of the tavern. An unstoppable force met an immovable object, and they collided, with sparks. They began to merge together, melting into one being, locking and intertwining around each other, engrossing themselves entirely in what made the other part of the equation tick. They knew without a fraction of doubt that they should be kissing. They knew they should be together. As quickly as it was happening, the moonlight had, after all, been reserved for them, and they knew they should take their chance to become better acquainted with each other's lips.

They knew they were two songbirds dancing under a shade of stars.

They didn't know Deryn had followed them out until she cleared her throat.

"*AGAIN?*" They cried, exasperated.

"AGAIN!" Roared the Prince like a hugely overgrown and distastefully bearded child being read a bedtime story, "TELL ME AGAIN HOW THE BASTARD'S GOING TO SUFFER!"

Leonard Garden-Hand stretched his neck and shoulders.

"Again, my lord?"

"YES. NOW."

"The thief will attempt to steal the sword this time," he moaned monotonously, "But will find it heavily guarded… And then they will find themselves on the chopping block."

The Prince laughed himself to sleep, falling eventually into a thunderous quietness, like the last fading roars of a victorious beast before the very end.

## Chapter Sixteen: Rest and Respite

The rest of the night passed without any major incidents.

Xiang escorted Patton back out of the forest, to Priestess Trinna's house. The others went to sleep elsewhere, in places Marian did not know about. The bard at the tavern stayed behind to finish the last of the night's roast potatoes. A man who had been admiring him from afar for weeks finally got the courage to approach him. After awkward confessions, they made a date, and the heavens opened.

Rain fell, as was regular, and it rattled against the windows of Marian's house as she sat alone, barefoot, with tea, thinking of the week ahead.

She thought that in the morning, the terms of the contest would almost definitely be announced. Also in the morning, Patton Cross would probably be arrested for the minor crimes he'd been committing. Thirdly, in the morning, she thought there was a slight chance she might meet with Aleta and find out exactly what she was doing.

There was a knock at the door. Confused, not expecting visitors, Marian cautiously stood and tentatively walked into the hallway. There was another knock, louder, more urgent. Slowly, softly, she opened the door.

Jemima gusted in.

"Sorry," she said, "I came as quickly as I could."

Marian looked her over. She was completely water-logged, her damp coat an even darker green than usual, and she was holding several bags.

"What's in the bags?"

"A shark," Jemima sighed exhaustedly, "Sorry. Snappy. It's… It's clothes."

"*Clothes?*" Marian asked, unconsciously removing Jemima's coat, "Well, I suppose that's good, you can change out of these… Fuck, Jemima. You're soaked."

Jemima's eyes widened. Marian met them with her own. They both blushed.

"Anyway," Marian moved on, as though this was the place it did not feel like quite the time, "What are they for?"

Jemima's blush seemed to intensify.

"I was hoping to stay here for the night."

"Oh."

There was a pause, Marian furrowing her brow slightly as she finally entirely unfastened Jemima's coat.

"Can I?" Jemima asked, shyly.

"It wasn't long ago that you broke in here, not caring whether I thought it was okay or not... And I attacked you. With a dagger."

Jemima looked down, and slumped her arms slightly.

"So obviously, yes. You can stay tonight."

Jemima looked up, and dropped her bags.

"Really? I can?"

"You stayed last night. Why not stay again?"

They hugged.

"No, no, no, hugging was a bad idea," Marian pulled away, "Now I'M soaked. Let's get you out of those clothes."

"Absolutely stop saying things like that unless you are saying them into my neck."

They pretended as though that particular thread of the conversation hadn't happened as Jemima went upstairs to change and Marian boiled the kettle, which, unsurprisingly, rumbled seductively. By the time Jemima came back down, Marian had prepared new cups of tea for both of them, and they sat on the couch, cuddling close to each other.

"Where do you…" Marian began.

"Why do you…" Jemima began.

"You first." They said simultaneously, and then laughed. Jemima went first.

"Why do you walk around barefoot?"

Marian laughed again, and spluttered, spitting out some of her tea.

"It's… It's just more comfortable. Is that the most important question?"

"Oh, and I suppose *your* question is *so* much more important."

"I was going to ask where you usually stay."

"I stay in the attic room, at Celinda's house. It's nice there, but it's nothing on home."

Jemima took a sip of her tea, and they listened to the rain for a while. Unprompted, Jemima began to elaborate.

"Home isn't far, really. I don't know if you've been to Dove's Rest, but it's this run-down little village a few miles inland. I used to live there with my grandmother. It's so dull there, and it smells… Peculiar. I've never been able to quite put my finger on the smell… But, anyway, that's where I lived. And one day, Robin Hood came to town."

Marian furrowed her brow.

"Or, I mean, Celinda and Deryn came to town. I was interested, because nobody usually visited. There was no reason to visit at all. So I followed them, and they… Stole things."

Marian sipped her tea.

"They started small, you know? Money, watches... But then they did something bigger. They went into the town hall... I say town hall, it was more of a glorified shed... And they took a book."

"A book?" Marian asked.

"A book. But a big book. Not a big book as in oh this book's really heavy, a big book as in an *important* book. It was a diary- the diary of an old mayor who'd died years and years ago. They say the day he died, the village changed, that nobody had the energy to keep it looking... Well, nice. Like a nice place to be. So it was pretty important that nobody take this book. It was kind of a relic, you know?"

Marian nodded.

"But they saw me, outside the building, in an alleyway, as they were shoving the book in a big old bag Deryn was carrying. It looked exciting, and I... Asked them if I could steal things too. Celinda said I didn't need permission to steal things, that that was going against the entire point of stealing."

Marian laughed quietly, leaning further into Jemima, rubbing lightly at her shoulder.

"But they said I could join them, if I proved I could actually steal things. And I opened my palm, and showed them a watch, and they said that didn't prove anything, but then I told Celinda to check her pockets."

"*You stole Celinda's watch?*" Marian asked with a completely undisguised tone of total admiration.

"Well, I have good reflexes. You remember when we fought."

"Like it was yesterday..." Marian said in plastic wistfulness.

"Oh, the good old days..." Jemima added, following suit in the joke, "But anyway. They said that was good, very good, but I had to do one more thing to prove my worth. And so, I stole the innkeeper's diamond ring..."

"I WAS THERE," Marian suddenly exploded. Jemima jumped, startled, almost spilling her tea over her legs, "DOVE'S REST. I was there. I was fucking there,

Jemima! I stayed in that Inn, it was awful, the bed was lumpy and everything smelled of beetroot…"

"BEETROT," Jemima shouted, mirroring Marian in volume, "IT SMELLED OF *BEETROOT*. That's the smell! That's absolutely the smell!"

They paused. They intended this pause to be brief, so that both of them could catch their breath, but it ended up going on for much longer than either of them had anticipated, as different iterations of the same gears turned in both of their heads.

"What we've established," clarified Marian, "Is that at some point I visited your home village just as you and two of the other Robins were stealing, and leaving."

"Yes." Jemima replied.

"Yes…" Marian repeated.

"Isn't that…"

"Really weird?"

"Yes."

"But sort of…"

"Absolutely amazing?"

"Yes."

"Yes."

The rain intensified outside, as did the presence of snails. They had been on a brief holiday while the sun had been out, but now it was firmly gone, they returned to roam the streets like a thousand tiny youths meandering around trying desperately to find something, anything, to take their minds off the monotone of life. A couple of them crossed the cobble road, and to any observers it would have looked completely deliberate. Gradually, they began to cover every surface again. Gravestones, fences, and posts, and quite a lot of them crawled up the walls of Marian's house, perhaps sensing that inside, there was an interesting moment of time, far from the touch of humanity and snails, in a numinous bubble between seconds.

The snails were entirely correct, as inside, life was anything but monotone. The two women had finished their tea, and had been swapping more stories. Jemima had just finished telling a humorous tale of how she stole a man's tie, a navy tie with an anchor print pattern, and sold it to his brother not five minutes later.

"Tell me something funny you've done!" Jemima requested, enthused.

"Well... The other night, when I didn't manage to rob the grave," Marian began, as Jemima sat cross-legged on the couch facing her, "I did manage to steal a hat... From a man's head."

Jemima cocked her head slightly to the side, and motioned for Marian to continue.

"That's... Sort of the end of the story. He was drunk, stumbling home from the Intoxicated Swan, and I took his watch, and then... His hat. From his head. I just reached up and took it."

Jemima raised a hand to her own face, resting a finger on her lips.

"I really like you, Marian." She said.

"I... Really like you too, Jemima." Marian replied.

"I'm sorry I broke into your house, and I'm sorry I got you caught by Trinna."

"I'm sorry I attacked you with a dagger."

"I'm... Sorry we didn't meet sooner."

"Things would have been different."

"We might even love each other by now."

"... Oh."

"I don't mean, as in... What I'm trying to say is that... Oh no. I'm sorry, that sounded weird. All I meant was..."

"Jemima."

"... Marian?"

"I'm going to politely ask you to not mention the concept of love for... Just a little while longer. I don't want to say it too early, because... The physical aspect of our relationship is... Wonderful. And you're... Wonderful. And I'm infatuated with you, certainly, I won't deny that I think you're the most precisely, perfectly, seamlessly beautiful girl, and that when I think of how quickly I've fallen for you, my heart races and my palms sweat... But I mean... Let's not... Yet... I don't want to ruin this..." Marian trailed off.

Jemima waited, not sure if Marian had ended her sentence.

"Do you really think I'm beautiful?" She asked.

Marian was startled.

"Well, of course I do. I told you so, last night. I seem to remember moaning it into your shoulder."

Jemima smiled and looked down at her hands.

"I thought you were just saying that because you liked how it sounded."

"I do like the way it sounds, but that doesn't mean it's not true. I like the way it's easy for me to say. I like how I don't have to put any effort into saying it, if that makes sense."

Jemima nodded, blushing down at her hands, fidgeting incessantly, trying to stop herself from exploding into both smiling and crying.

"I like how... I can just... Say it. I can say... You're beautiful, Jemima."

Jemima burst. Tears streamed down her face, her mouth opened into a bright, wide smile, and she threw her arms around Marian's neck, burying her head in her shoulder and openly, happily weeping.

"I'm sorry! I'm sorry," she said between sobs, "I don't mean to cry, it's just… This is going to sound so predictable and silly but I don't think anybody's ever called me that before, and I, it's, it's even better coming from you, because I think you're amazing, and I really just… You're beautiful too, Marian."

Marian smiled, now struggling to hold back tears herself. They sat locked together for some time. Marian managed to force back her tears, and Jemima cried all of hers down the side of Marian's sleeve.

They separated, and made eye contact, and burst into laughter. They hugged, and kissed softly. They remained close, the tips of their noses touching.

"Now?" Jemima asked, her voice only just audible.

"Definitely not. Still too early. It's literally been less than two minutes since I said that." Marian replied.

"True. Yeah, you're right. Sorry."

"One day soon, though."

"Definitely."

They had not known each other for long, but they knew this for certain.

# Chapter Seventeen: A Trial by Chess

The citizens of Knottwood speak of a man named Patton Cross.

They talk of his villainous deeds, of his cowardly feats, of his simply no-good exploits. They talk of how this man, this fallen, decaying, *black* soldier, keeps stealing from the rich. They speak of his unknowable accomplice, and of his head's disappointing position at the top of his torso, and they take extra care to mention the colour of his skin. They speak of him in whispers as he walks by. They speak of him in shouted cries, some of which are expressed through rotten fruit as it is propelled through the air. They speak of him in The Intoxicated Swan.

The citizens are, as is to be expected, unequivocally racist.

Sitting in the town square, across from the stone tower that assaults the skyline and makes the clouds uncomfortable, facing the fountain, and with a wonderful view of any executions that might theoretically happen at some point, are the barracks. Today, an exhausted sun glances down every so often through gaps in lethargic clouds. The sky is lazy, and the sun wishes more than anything to go back to bed. A specific guard steps outside.

He is closely followed by another. They talk for a while about anything and everything except the inevitable. They are as tired as the sun, but as the one on the right reminds the one on the left, they are sworn by duty to arrest Patton Cross. Their conversation gradually shifted to the past tense.

"Were you serious?" The guard on the left asked.

"About what?" Responded the guard on the right.

"Sailing," explained the guard on the left, moving out of the way of a worried-looking father in formal attire dragging his son behind him, "When you said we could sail… Were you serious?"

"I don't know," The guard on the right said shortly after he dodged out of the way of a woman walking eight dogs, all of which wanted to go in different directions, "I mean, yeah. D'you want to?"

"Yeah. I do."

"Me too."

"Shall we?"

"Yeah."

"Really?"

"Yeah."

"Okay."

"Okay."

They delivered this part of the conversation in rapid staccato as they dodged through a group of young adults who weren't looking where they were going, and they reached the dock road. From here, they could see the Church spires standing in proud devotion, reaching up to the sky and appealing to a greater power, and they knew that sitting in humble solitude behind it was Priestess Trinna's house, and they knew that sitting in humble solitude inside it was Patton Cross, and they knew exactly what they had to do.

They turned, and walked down the road to the docks, booked passage on the next boat overseas, and went home to pack.

Sir Patton Cross sat alone in Trinna's house while Trinna herself delivered a sermon at the Church. He had never been much for sermons.

When nobody came to arrest him, he risked walking outside into the garden, half expecting an angry mob at his door. An organ in the Church began to play a tune he almost liked.

He thought of the plan he had made with Aleta, and he leaned on the fence of Trinna's garden in regret, not at all sure if it had done anything worthwhile. He thought it over, and in the time it took for a single snail to slime its way across a rock across the way, he had not reached a veritable conclusion. Certainly, thanks to his assorted misdemeanours, nobody would now suspect Quilla. Nobody would see Quilla in the street and assume she stole the axe, for now everybody knew that it was Patton. That much was a positive. But from what Xiang said, Quilla was not holding up well.

A small breeze brushed through the bristles of his hair, and he rather missed his hat.

He wondered where his hat had gone. He didn't dare go back to the Intoxicated Swan to look for it now. He thought back to the night before his execution, when he had what he thought was going to be the last drink of his life.

"Four beers, please." He had said.

"Certainly, my good man," the bartender had replied, "Would you like them all individually or would you like me to pull them at once into one huge, nigh-impossible four-pint tankard? At that point you may as well have just brought a bucket."

The bartender was joking, and Patton laughed because he needed to, before sitting at a table in the corner with four beers in front of him, and beginning to throw them down his throat with barely a chance for them to linger in his mouth. He didn't want to taste it. He just wanted to feel it.

People turned and whispered, but acted like they didn't know who he was. After the first beer, he knew they knew. After the second, he knew they knew he knew. After the third, he knew very little.

When he spilled the fourth on his coat, he knew he had had too much, and he stood, and staggered out.

Now that he thought about it, he hadn't taken off his hat the entire time. Somewhere between the Swan and his house, he must have dropped it, or else it was stolen. But who would have the sheer audacity to steal a hat from somebody's head?

"This was the hat, then?" asked Jemima, picking up a hat in Marian's house and trying it on in front of the mirror.

Marian looked up as she pulled on her boots.

"Yes," she confirmed, "But don't wear it out. It's disrespectful."

"Oh but stealing it was perfectly fine?" Jemima teased.

"Don't act like you don't steal things for a living too," Marian teased in response as she laced her boots, "Now come on. I want to get into the town square as quickly as possible."

Jemima was still modelling the hat in the mirror. Marian stood and swiped it from her head.

"Hey!" Jemima cried, turning and trying to grab the hat back before laughing loudly, "Okay, that's twice you've stolen the same hat now."

"Come on." Marian smiled, dragging Jemima towards the front door and practically shoving her out of it. They were outside, at last, in the bleary fog of the day that hadn't had enough sleep.

"Is there a reason why you chose to live this close to a graveyard?" Jemima asked, as they walked to the square.

"Convenience. I don't want to have to carry anything I steal all the way across town."

"But then isn't it more dangerous to live this close? I mean, if somebody caught you…"

They opened the door to a general store named Watford and Son. The door had been newly installed a few days prior, and it rang a small bell as they entered. Jemima and Marian kept talking as they browsed, and stole, miscellaneous items. The whole store had an overwhelming smell of burning bread, which was perhaps why the store owner was nowhere to be seen. Jemima picked up a bag of flour and dropped it squarely into a satchel over her shoulder.

"… Wouldn't the guards think to check the houses closest to the graveyard before anywhere else?" Jemima finished her question and kept her satchel open as Marian gently placed in a box of half a dozen eggs, above the bag of flour, so they would not break. An egg mess is the worst kind of mess to have in a satchel.

"That's why I don't get caught."

"Well, you sort of do…"

"That was *your* fault!"

They smiled at each other, and left the store. The owner walked back in just after they left, holding a plate of burned bread, thinking the smell must have driven away potential customers. He wished that there was a different way to cook individual slices of bread as opposed to holding them above an open flame. Some sort of alternate method that was less likely to scorch one's bread would be ideal, he thought, as he took a despondent bite of what at this point could not legally be considered a viable breakfast.

They arrived at the town square. It was as busy as ever, despite the laziness of the day. As groggy as everybody seemed to be, they would not be swayed from their ambitions. They had risen early, as was the standard to which they promised themselves they would live by, and they would make the most of the day at any cost.

Jemima and Marian watched as the town crier left the guard barracks with a list of news and current events to proclaim to the citizens. They watched him walk across the town square, everybody moving out of his way without needing to be asked. They watched him clear his throat.

"HEAR YE ALL," he broadcast, the sharp "REGARDING THE CONTEST TAKING PLACE ON THE THIRTEENTH OF THE MONTH… TERMS WILL BE STATED. THE CONTEST WILL BE IN FIVE PARTS… FIRSTLY, A TRIAL BY FIRE…"

*Fire?* Marian thought.

"SECONDLY AND THIRDLY, TWO TRIALS OF COMBAT…"

"Against who…?" Jemima whispered.

"FOURTHLY, A TRIAL OF ARCHERY… AND FIFTHLY, CHESS."

"Chess, are you serious?" a passer-by asked, "Fucking chess? Fire, combat, archery and *chess?*"

The town crier nodded.

"For fuck's sake. What, couldn't you think of anything else, or is the Prince just that fucking pretentious? Like is he sat up there right now practicing? What an absolute c…"

The Chief of the guard placed his hand firmly on the passer-by's shoulder. The passer-by gulped, nodded, and joined the crowd again. The Chief slid another small scroll into the crier's hand, who nodded, read it over, and cleared his throat again.

"A FINAL ANNOUNCEMENT…" he said.

"IF ANYBODY HAS SEEN TWO GUARDS…" he continued to say.

"BY THE NAMES OF CUNNINGHAM AND PRICE…" he further said.

"LET THEM KNOW THAT LEONARD GARDEN-HAND SAYS… THEY'RE FIRED." He concluded.

"They're probably playing chess somewhere." Mumbled a passer-by.

Up in the tower, the Prince practiced chess with a servant. He moved his rightmost pawn two spaces forward, the servant moved their queenside pawn two spaces forward, the prince moved his leftmost pawn two spaces forward and the servant moved their queenside bishop in front of their kingside pawn, to which the Prince scoffed as he moved his left rook to the space behind his leftmost pawn.

The servant moved their king forward into the space previously occupied by their queenside pawn, and the Prince, seemingly focusing mainly on symmetry, moved his right rook forward to mirror the position of his left rook.

The servant moved the bishop they had in play and took the Prince's rook.

"FUCK." Roared the Prince. The servant resisted a smile.

The Prince moved his right knight to take the bishop, and the servant moved their king backwards, to the space on opposite side of the queen to the one it had started on. The Prince moved his queenside pawn two spaces forward, and the servant moved their previously kingside pawn one space forward.

The Prince put his queen into play, moving it two spaces forward, and the servant instantly countered this by moving their remaining bishop into the perfect position to place the Prince's king in check.

"ABSOLUTELY SHITTING FUCK." The Prince bellowed.

The Prince moved his king one space to his left, and the servant moved their bishop diagonally one space to their right, taking the Prince's bishop, which the Prince took with his other knight.

The servant moved their queen to take the Prince's rightmost pawn. The Prince, in a half-baked revenge attempt, moved his own queen and took the pawn furthest to the servant's left... Which was of course taken by the servant's rook.

"OH YOU TOTAL BUGGERING ARSEWIPE."

The Prince moved his left knight forwards, and the servant moved their rightmost pawn one space forward, possibly with the intent to take the knight diagonally, to which the Prince responded by moving his knight into "safety", which meant straight in front of the servant's other rook.

"CHECK!" The Prince shouted.

The servant moved their rook forward and took the knight.

"FUCK. FUCK, FUCK, FUCK. WHY ARE YOU EVEN ALLOWED CASTLES? YOU'RE FUCKING POOR. I ACTUALLY LIVE IN ONE."

The Prince moved his knight around the servant's queen, which the servant proceeded to move diagonally to the space in front of the Prince's right bishop.

Panicking, the Prince moved his king one space forwards. The servant moved their left rook to the Prince's right corner, the Prince moved his king another space forward, the servant took the Prince's right bishop with their rook, the Prince moved his king one space left and the servant took the Prince's left bishop, the Prince moved his king back one space diagonally to get into position to take the rook…

The servant moved their queen diagonally towards the Prince and once again placed him into check.

"YOU SHOULDN'T… YOU SHOULDN'T BE FUCKING ALLOWED TO KNOW ABOUT THIS. POOR PEOPLE SHOULDN'T *KNOW* THINGS."

The Prince moved his king one space forward again, and the servant moved their queen diagonally backwards to a position where the Prince was once again in check.

The Prince moved his king back towards himself again, and the servant moved their queen in a way that simultaneously took the Prince's right knight and put the Prince in check yet again.

The Prince moved the king one space forward, and the servant moved their piece one space to their right, putting the Prince in check once more. He moved his king one space left, and the servant used their queen to take the pawn one space behind his king. He motioned to take the queen, but realised he would be immediately taken by the rook, so he moved the Prince diagonally forwards to the left, and the servant took another pawn, chasing the king, which was moved another space diagonally forwards to the left…

The servant moved their right knight two spaces forwards and one to their left.

"Checkmate…" They said.

"… Fuck off." The Prince said, surprisingly calmly.

"I'm sorry?" The servant asked.

"FUCK OFF!" he screamed. The servant stood, bowed, and left the room, pushing past Leonard Garden-Hand, the Chief of the Guard, who had entered at some point during the game.

"This is fucking ridiculous." The king's brother said to the Chief.

"Let's try again, yes?" Leonard said. The Prince grumbled as Leonard set the pieces of the board back up.

The Prince moved the pawn in front of his right bishop one space forward. The Chief moved his kingside pawn two spaces forward. The Prince moved the pawn in front of his right knight forward two spaces. The Chief moved his queen diagonally, landing next to the second pawn the Prince had moved.

"Checkmate." Chief Leonard said.

"...How the fuck?"

Chief Leonard calmly packed away the pieces as the Prince stared dumbfounded at the table. Leonard handed the box to another servant, who left the room, following the first servant who had gone downstairs to their quarters.

"My lord, now we are done with chess, there is news."

The Prince remained staring at the table.

"The two guards I sent to arrest Patton Cross in preparation for the contest have vanished."

"Then fire them," the Prince said in a voice barely above a whimper as he broke his trance and looked around the room instead of affixing his gaze on the table, "Fire the bastards."

"I have done so, sir."

"Good... Good."

"Should I arrest him myself then, sir?"

The Prince waved his hand, a gesture which Leonard took to mean yes, definitely. He nodded, and left the room, leaving the Prince alone at an empty table, baffled at his two consecutive chess losses.

The gears of the day needed oiling, but still they turned. Outside, Jemima and Marian were on their way home, stopping only to pilfer some milk, while

Patton Cross watched and waited for either Trinna or some guards to come and make dinner or arrest him. Inside, two guards who lived in neighbouring houses both packed suitcases to leave in the morning. The one on the left, Cunningham, shined his shoes in preparation while the one on the right, Price, folded several shirts.

An innocent but frustrated passer-by walked away from the town square towards a park, but was stopped along the way by a woman in a green coat.

## Chapter Eighteen: The Storm, Part One

The rain decided it meant business, and began to lash its fury down on the Earth.

It pushed away the slothful fog of the day, washing away lethargy as though it were a loose stain, and it brought with it an influx of snails. In the town square, a ring of snails arrived on the fountain, following each other in an endless loop, like children playing chase in a field. Except in this instance, the field was a fountain and all the children were snails. Children are not usually snails.

In the park on the opposite side of town to the graveyard, a passer-by passed by, after a long conversation. He dodged snails making silver threads along the ground in possibly the strangest game of hopscotch that has ever happened, and finally made his way out of the park, and back home. He lived in a house that was precisely the average house, which suited him as he was precisely the average passer-by, and as he settled on his average couch and his average husband settled down next to him to begin another long conversation, something more important happened elsewhere.

Aleta walked in the opposite direction, almost invisible under the sensory overload of green that was the park, which she exited. On the opposite side of town to almost everything, the houses were poorer and so were the people. Aleta much preferred it here. She preferred the old wooden houses, she preferred the old wooden people, and she preferred the general old wooden aesthetic. This was a good place, and she walked straight through it, head held high despite the rain trying to force it down.

Eventually she reached an old house, and knocked on the door. It was a very specific knock- two long knocks, one short knock, and two long knocks again. The rain made a chorus of tiny knocks behind her, and from inside she heard the dull knocks of a slow-moving human making their way down the stairs.

An old man opened a small hatch on the front of the door, peering through with one eye, the skin around which was mostly made of wrinkle.

"Do you want to play a chess game?" Aleta asked, and the man began to fiddle with the lock as something equally as important happened elsewhere.

Marian and Jemima were baking a cake. They had decided to bake a cake that day, and that is what they were doing, as two consenting adults who saw an idea and followed it to fruition. They were on a journey, together, as two women, heavily infatuated with each other, but also heavily infatuated in a different sort of way with the concept of cake. They had realised their mutual fondness for cake, subsequently realised they had the capacity to make their own cake, and finally realised that if they simply stole some ingredients they could come home and make as much cake as they felt comfortable with.

They both felt comfortable with at least twice the recommended amount of cake, and that is exactly what they were making.

"Butter?" Marian asked.

"Got it." Jemima replied.

"Flour?"

"Got it."

"Cocoa powder?"

"Resisting urge to taste."

"Salt?"

"Not resisting urge to taste."

"… Salt?"

"… Got it."

"Eggs?"

"Got it."

"Vanilla extract?"

"Oh! Do you know the café in Dove's Rest? I worked there for a while, and there was a time…"

"Tell me later. Vanilla extract, Jemima?"

"Got it!"

"Buttermilk?"

"Got it."

"Baking powder?"

"Got it…"

"Sugar?"

"What IS baking powder?"

"Sugar?"

"No, sugar's a separate thing! Baking powder seems like… I don't know. It's an odd thing, isn't it?"

"Sugar?"

"Oh! Sorry. Got it!"

Marian smiled, and Jemima smiled in response, though slightly wider and more quickly than she intended. She forced back her smile into wherever she had drawn it from and stood stoic in front of Marian. She paused for a second, and nodded solemnly. Marian watched this entire emotional transition from beginning to end, enraptured, and taken aback at Jemima's ability to shift so quickly.

Marian held eye contact with Jemima, who stood rigid. Marian slowly picked up a teaspoon between her right thumb and index finger, scooped out a small amount of cocoa powder from the bowl on the kitchen counter, and gradually edged it towards Jemima's face.

Jemima stayed still, indomitable. She would not be swayed by a spoonful of cocoa.

Marian struggled to hold back a laugh as the spoon reached Jemima's lips, pushing against them slightly, parting them the tiniest fraction. Jemima responded by tightening them instantly.

"Come on," Marian whispered, staring Jemima down, "*Open up.*"

Jemima's hand twitched. Marian noticed, and pushed the spoon ever so slightly further forward.

Jemima opened her mouth, reached up, grabbed Marian's hand, and pushed the spoon the final distance. She immediately choked on the cocoa powder, and spluttered, gagging and spitting. Marian let go of the spoon at the same time Jemima did, and it clattered to the floor as Marian turned and poured a glass of water.

"*Open up.*" Marian repeated, softer this time, gently placing the rim of the glass to Jemima's mouth.

After a minute, Jemima had recovered, though her eyes watered slightly.

"I'm sorry, I've spat cocoa powder all over your floor."

Marian shrugged.

"It's totally fine. I'm sorry, actually," she said, "That was far too much cocoa powder for anybody to swallow that quickly."

"It's okay. I didn't think I was that bad at swallowing." Jemima said entirely innocently.

Marian washed a spoon. She stopped for a moment, turned, shook her head and then turned back, continuing to wash a spoon.

"Let's just... Bake a cake."

They began to bake a cake, and they spoke as they did so. Mixing ingredients, occasionally tasting ingredients, and beginning to tell stories, which are, in a way, made of ingredients.

"I was wondering... Do you know anything about Deryn?" Marian asked.

"Well, yes," Jemima replied, "Like what?"

"As in, what's her whole sort of situation? Why doesn't she speak the same language as us? It's fine that she does. I'm just confused."

"I think it's a choice. She certainly understands ours. Maybe it's a kind of… Intentionally confusing hobby!"

"A what?"

"I mean to say, maybe she's doing it on purpose just so we'll ask this question."

"That seems frighteningly pointless."

"Well then maybe it's something to do with her past! Maybe the language is important to her."

"Do you know anything about her past?"

Jemima thought for a moment as the kettle rumbled seductively. Pouring tea, she finally responded.

"Celinda told me once that Deryn used to live on an Island? I think it was to the south, but something awful happened and she moved back here…"

"Something awful," Marian hummed to herself, "A traumatic event, then? A harsh situation that lead to a radical change of perspective?"

## Chapter Nineteen: The Storm, Part Two

Many seasons had passed on the Island to the south. The old woman's hair, the air that blew through it, and the wooden chair on which she sat- all were seasoned. As she looked out to sea, drops of water would land on her cheek, sending a chill down her neck, but still she sat and she looked out. It was grey today. That was the only word to describe the weather- grey.

She used to favour a spot near the top of the mountain inland, but for reasons that came with seasons, she found a new place to set her chair. Along the shoreline was her favourite place to sit now. It was peaceful there. Sometimes she would fish. Most of the time, she would not. But always, she carried her rod and her fishing knife, never knowing when the urge to catch would overtake her. The rod rested next to her chair, the knife lay idly on her lap. Her grip on the sides of the chair grew tighter as the wind grew stronger.

She would not fish today. The story, her story, was not about fishing.

Down from the rocks near the beach, her daughter approached. She was a younger woman dressed more warmly with a youthful vigour in her step- or maybe less of a youthful vigour and more an immediate and important concern. Her stride was firm and deliberate, her leather boots sank into the sand at every step towards her father, and her hair billowed behind her in the stubborn wind. There was sand in her eye, which she instinctively rubbed, though an echoed memory in the back of her head told her rubbing would only make it worse. No matter, she thought.

The two women were side by side now. The younger of the two looked down expectantly, but the gaze of the elder was set firmly out over the sea. Shifting awkwardly, the younger woman cleared her throat, but still to no avail. It wasn't that the old woman hadn't noticed her. She just wasn't ready to look away from the sea.

Bored of waiting, the daughter spoke.

"Ma?" she said, though a gust of wind screamed at the same time, rendering her inaudible. She tried again, "Ma."

"Hm?" the old woman responded, her stare unwavering.

"Where's Paula?"

There was silence, except for the wind. More sand flew into the daughter's eyes, and she looked down and rubbed them again. Her vision was blurred for just a moment, then it focused on the older woman's sandals.

"Rubbing them is just going to make them worse." the old woman said in the tone of somebody saying something that has been said too many times, lifting her head slightly as if to roll her eyes, but still not looking away from the sea.

"I know, Ma," the daughter said, all the impatience of a girl half her age, "But where's Paula?"

Paula was the daughter's niece, the old woman's granddaughter, and she was missing. She had been gone since the morning, running out as usual down the rocky path to the beach to find the most interesting shells possible before going up the mountain for berries. The night before, there had been a storm, which the daughter slept through quite easily, though a few of many rumbles of thunder woke her every so often. She told Paula to be careful running up and down the Island, not wanting her to slip on a rock covered in rain, and now she couldn't find her.

The old woman still didn't answer.

"Ma, I understand if you're tired. I woke up a few times in the night too, I can't imagine how the storm must've been for you. But I need to know where Paula is. I went up as far as she's allowed on the mountain and saw no sign of her. Is she down here, somewhere along the beach?"

"The storm?"

This was annoying.

The younger woman crouched down to the elder's level, lowering her voice to a couple of rungs above a whisper on the ladder of volume.

"Listen. Ma. This is serious. I'm worried, she's never done this before. Have you. Seen her. Since. This morning?" She punctuated her words by tapping on the arm of the old woman's chair.

"What storm?" replied the old woman absently. The younger woman stood back up, waving her arms in impatience, her voice loud and angry now.

"The storm! Last night! The thunder, you know thunder? Don't tell me you've forgotten what thunder is. Look, you've got your knife and your rod but you've forgotten to do any fishing!"

The old woman furrowed her brow, contemplating and considering what her daughter was saying, but all the while still staring out over the water.

"Stop ignoring me, you old fool! Where is my daughter? Is this some game of hide and seek you're playing because I DON'T WANT TO PL-"

"She has been spared."

Wind. Wind and tide. The tide, a waxing lilt, the wind a discordant whine. A small ray of sunshine pierced through the clouds, but nobody noticed. The young woman looked at the old woman looking out to sea, and neither of them at anything else.

"What?"

"She has been spared," the old woman declared authoritatively and calmly, as deliberate as striding along a beach in leather boots but with a sense of resigned inevitability, "From what the storm brings."

"Spared from what the...?" the daughter questioned, anger turning to confusion, "What are you talking about? What does that mean? Are- Are you... Where's Paula?"

She clung to this question like a life raft.

"I've spared her. It was this, or let her burn."

The word "this" caught the young woman's attention. This? The knife, the wind, the chair, the sea?

The sea. Sand blew in the daughter's eyes.

She rubbed them, instinctively, turning to face the same direction as her mother. Her vision was blurred for a moment, but then adjusted, to a beam of the sun's light falling softly on a rock formation. She noticed now another sound, separate from the wind and the tide. It was rope.

It was rope.

She was hanging from it. Swinging, backwards and forwards like the tide.

The old woman stared.

"Did you notice, perhaps, my daughter, that the higher points of the island were slightly warmer today?"

Rope. Swinging. Paula. Hanged.

"The noises you heard in the night were no storm."

Wind. Tide. Rope.

"I have lived a long life. I have sat in many places and caught so very many fish. I only hanged her because after everything I've seen, I didn't want to have to see what my knife would do to her."

They both stared out to sea.

"So I spared her."

The old woman looked away, standing and facing her daughter. The ground began to rumble. In time, it would shake more. There would be noise, and heat, and sulphur.

"It's today, my daughter. It erupts today, and you should leave. You should go, Deryn. You should go. See the world, before it ends."

Tide.

"I've seen so many things. I didn't want her to see... I spared her. If you would like, girl, if you don't want to leave... I could spare you too."

Wind.

As she looked out to sea, a drop of water hit the daughter's cheek, sending a chill down her neck. She left the Island later that day and never looked back.

The carriage was late. Very late. Six months late. Sitting in Dove's Rest was a young woman- Deryn, of course. She had been waiting for the carriage. It had, as usual, proved to be a let-down. She thought she'd give it one more month and then try and find a horse to steal.

She thought of six months ago. She thought of death, of destruction, of the end of the world. There was nothing to do now but wait for a carriage to take her somewhere safe. Somewhere where nothing died. There was, quite suddenly, a noise. It was the noise she was expecting, the noise she was hoping for. It wasn't the clattering of hooves or the turning of wooden wheels. It was her sister, approaching with today's breakfast.

"Good feast today," said her sister, "Really good stuff."

"Thank the Gods for that." Deryn responded.

Her sister sat next to her, handing her the spoils of the morning. They picked a few grey feathers from their meal and carelessly tossed them aside. They had no need for feathers. Of all the things that had become totally meaningless in the last six months, feathers were top of the list. Of course, however, lists were not far behind feathers.

They ate their meat in silence. There was little to talk about. They finished the meat and threw away the bones.

"I've been thinking," Her sister said at last, "That we should probably leave this carriage business. Where's it even going to go?"

"We'll find our Aunt."

"Our Aunt isn't the answer. We should go somewhere else. We need change."

"Really? You're going there again? Look, the carriage will be here. The man says that it'll be here in five minutes."

"The carriage has been expected in five minutes for six months."

"I just don't think it's worth stopping waiting now! We've waited so long. If we leave now, I bet it'll come. It'll come as soon as we leave."

"Honestly, Deryn, I think you put too much stock in the notion of this carriage. We should go somewhere else. At least take a look outside. When was the last time you did?"

She thought about it. She remembered with ease. The last time she had been outside was, in fact, six months ago. She had arrived at Dove's Rest and gone straight to the inn and never left.

The events were burned into her memory with the literal fire around her. She imagined the fire had gone out since, but at the time there was no sign of it ever stopping. The fire consumed everything. It WAS everything. Buildings burned, the air burned... People burned.

She ran from the Island- or rather sailed, though she would have ran if it were possible- and she found her sister. Everything else was gone- the world had ended, and nothing meant anything anymore, except for waiting for an unseen carriage.

A feather drifted back onto her lap. Absent-mindedly she thanked nothing and nobody in particular.

She sighed and turned to her sister, her first eye contact in a while. "Where would we go?"

"Anywhere. Just come with me, outside, and we'll work it out from there."

Reluctantly, the woman stood up. Her legs almost gave out underneath her, but her sister held her arm and kept her going. They exited, down the broken stairs and out.

Everything was filthy. Destruction was quite literally common as muck. After her eyes adjusted to the light, she glanced around. She saw nobody and nobody saw her.

There was no fire here. Perhaps nothing was burning anywhere any more. She wondered when it had stopped- for all she knew, it had only stopped five minutes ago.

"Come on, now. It's time to go." her sister squeezed her arm and they walked towards nowhere and nothing.

Then, quite suddenly, there was another squeeze. Somebody else had her arm.

"Deryn?

This voice was not familiar. This was a different voice. She had heard many voices in the past six months but not this one. This voice seemed to think that names were important.

"Deryn. Come with me. It's your Aunt."

There was an argument, and Deryn's sister left, leaving her with her Aunt, after only just convincing her to step outside. She had tried her best, but not succeeded, and she fled.

Her Aunt took her back inside, back into the Inn, and taught her a language that only they would understand.

Celinda had found Deryn.

## Chapter Twenty: The Storm, Part Three

Shortly after recounting the story, the cake was ready. It was a beautiful cake, all things considered. In this time of danger, and of uncertainty, and of the imminent possibility of death, it was nice to have cake.

They told more stories, and outside, the rain told its own. It battered the Earth, fistfuls of water smacking against rooftops as though houses were punching bags. The night was drowning under the barrage of precipitation, but Marian and Jemima did not notice.

The topic of conversation shifted to written stories.

"This whole writer thing," Jemima puzzled, twirling a corner of a slice of cake, "Do you ever think about actually doing it?"

Marian nodded and gestured to the set of drawers on the other side of the room.

"I've actually written things," She admitted, "I'll never publish them, but there all in there."

Jemima dropped her fork and clapped her hands.

"You have to read to me!"

"I'm not sure about that."

"No, please! Come on!"

Marian considered it. She'd never read her work aloud before, or even shown anybody the written pieces. She feared most people would hate her work. But Jemima was, at the end of the day, Jemima. She wasn't most people.

"Okay," Marian conceded, standing and walking to the drawer, "Here's something I wrote. It's... Well, I hope you like it." Marian pulled open a drawer and fished out a leather-bound maroon notebook, sat back down on the couch and began to read aloud.

*"I keep hearing people say that God works in mysterious ways. I don't quite know what that means, and I don't quite know who God is, but what I do know is what all the books in school told me- the mystery can always be solved, and the villain is usually an old man in a mask.*

*My dad says that I probably shouldn't ask people about God's motivations right now and that I should leave it all alone to focus on school. He says I'm very clever- that God made me clever. Mum doesn't say anything really.*

*But isn't the point of being clever to learn things? When I'm in school I read the books really quickly. There's a rack of books for my year and I've finished them all and had to move up to the books for next year. Dad says he's proud of me, but the school are "short-sighted", which means that they can't see the future and if I read all of next year's books now then they won't have any books for me next year. Like I said, mum says... Nothing. But regardless, if I'm clever, I should be learning things and therefore I should be looking for what God's doing and why He's doing it, because if God is biggest thing in the universe then His mysterious ways are the biggest thing to learn.*

*My teacher doesn't agree though. I asked her a question about God today. I asked her if she's ever met God and she said that she hasn't, and then she told me to go back to my seat before I could ask another. I don't understand that. I don't understand why a teacher would do that. Teachers are meant to teach things and if I'm asking them about something that means I want to be taught about it. I'm not going to learn anything if I'm just sat in my seat listening to somebody talk, like how mum mostly just sits there staring at people walk by talking at each other for hours and hours.*

*That's why I don't like church either. It's just sitting and listening. After a while I get distracted and start pulling threads out of the jumper dad makes me wear and he says to stop it because I'll ruin it but he shouldn't have told me that because I hate the jumper and ruining it would be brilliant. We were at church the other day. They kept talking about God and what He does but they never said why He does it, only that He works in mysterious ways. I asked dad why God's a He and why He couldn't be a girl and dad told me to be quiet, but I poked his leg until he answered and he said that on the eighth day God decided to be a boy and He's God so we can't argue. Mum was crying and I said sorry because I've been learning about social cues and I know that when people are sad you're meant to say sorry.*

*I don't understand why God would choose to be a boy. Boys are rubbish. Girls do much stronger things. I think God should have been a girl. We were meant to be having a girl around the house. Another one apart from me and mum that is. I asked dad where little girls come from and he said mum would go to a doctor and come back with a little girl. Mum was away with the doctor for a while though and then she came back without another girl and I don't understand that. That's when people started telling me God works in mysterious ways but that doesn't make sense. I want to find out why God does things and find out why He would do something that made my mum sad.*

*I think God should say sorry."*

"Oh my Gods," Jemima gasped, "That last line."

Marian's cheeks decided to blush, a pastime they had become quite fond of recently. She tried to speak, but words had apparently gone on holiday.

"I'm serious- but... Is that based on reality?"

Marian shook her head.

"Okay, well that's good- It would be horrible if that happened to you. But as a writer, I'm... Kind of... Shamed. By how you can make it seem so real if it didn't actually happen!"

Marian furrowed her brow.

"As a writer?" She asked, closing her notebook and placing it down on the edge of the couch in her living room. They were both sat on this couch, with crossed legs, plates of cake in their laps.

It was Jemima's turn to blush now. To an outside observer looking in, the amount of times these two women had blushed over the course of the past week or thereabouts might seem odd, but in their own private reality, Jemima and Marian barely noticed.

"I write too," Jemima explained in a voice that gave away how nervous about this she was, "But it isn't really the same sort of thing? It's a kind of study, or a... I don't know. Celinda describes it as a verbal museum, but that sounds pretentious. It's just real, I write about actual things."

"So it's non-fiction?" Marian asked, leaning closer, excited to hear about Jemima's writing.

"... Yes? Is that the term for things that aren't made up?" Jemima asked, and cocked her head slightly as Marian nodded, "Okay, well then, that's what I write. The most recent piece is... About you."

"Me?"

"Yes."

"What about me?"

"Well, your house."

"What about my house?"

"Well... Your bedroom."

"What about my bedroom?"

"About what it looks like."

"Can I... See?"

Jemima hesitated, but then pulled a folded piece of paper from her pocket, cleared her throat, and read aloud.

*"It is the bedroom of an eccentric. Nothing really fits with anything else individually but everything comes together into the most perfect mess, as if somebody has emptied out a hundred different jigsaw puzzles and tried to put them all together into one. It is the bedroom of a child, it is the bedroom of an adult, it is affected eclecticism of the highest degree, it is everything and nothing at once.*

*Depending on the length of your legs, this bedroom is between four and twenty strides. At a push, it could be from three to twenty-three. The ceiling is high- or low, depending on what angle you view it from- and the carpet is definitely a carpet, except in the corners and along the skirting boards where it doesn't seem to be quite so sure of itself, and the areas of mystery, the patches shrouded in the shadows of miscellanea carelessly strewn across the floor like constellations of paint from a thick brush flicked blindly over a canvas. Nobody knows if there's carpet underneath those things. Context clues would imply it but it's impossible to be sure.*

*The bed is immaculately dishevelled. Enough sheets to make a viable sail for a small vessel, more pillows than could ever be necessary, and a frankly ridiculous amount of blankets, a physical representation of total disorder. The bed is perfect for everything. The bed is perfect for a night alone, the bed is perfect for the fiftieth consecutive night alone, the bed is perfect for entertaining visitors on the fifty-first night, the bed is perfect for seeking the warmth of your own personal sun at the end of a walk with the moon, the bed is perfect for throwing yourself into the wind and letting the reckless abandon of a thunderstorm strike your skin like lightning, the bed is perfect for living in and loving in and most of all the bed is absolutely irrefutably perfect for sleeping in. Which is probably why it looks like it hasn't been made properly in weeks."*

Marian listened intently throughout, and then there was silence. It was the silence of a positive review, but an awkward silence for Jemima nonetheless.

"What did you... Think?"

"I liked it," Marian said sincerely, "You've got a gift, I think, but... My room isn't as messy as you imply..."

"Well, no, but, I sort of embellish the non-fiction so it's more interesting to read, and... I have a gift?"

"Yes! Absolutely. I'd argue that you're better than me at this."

"Oh, no, don't. Don't! Don't at all. That simply isn't true, you're not being fair to yourself, love."

"Love?"

"... It's a nice word. I don't mean to say I love you."

There was silence, but not for long.

"Unless I... Do?" Jemima asked, in the manner of somebody who has been presented with a question in a difficult class and thinks they may know the right answer but is not sure whether or not it would be a better option to sit in silence and provide no answer.

"Do you?" Marian asked in much the same way.

"Do you still think it's too early?"

"Do *you*?"

"I..."

"Do you just want to both say what we think at the same time?"

"... Yes?"

"Okay. On three."

Three.

Two.

One.

"It's about time." They said, in unison. Their voices were the same lettered note, but different pitches. Then, the hum of the note fading away like the last pound of a key on the world's most priceless piano, there was a beautiful silence. The sort of silence when both people know what is happening without the need for words, but don't know what to do about it without using the words.

The sort of silence that comes before a moment.

"Fuck this, Marian. I love you."

"I love you too, Jemima. Fuck this."

They kissed. Their lips locked together like two planets crashing into each other after millennia of passively but threateningly orbiting each other in a celestial stalemate. Their tongues met, and greeted each other with polite words, and then stronger words, and then almost swear words. They pulled apart, and one set of lips fell deliberately onto the other person's neck. They kissed in as many places as they could reach, as their fingers grazed the other's as though they were attached to the hands of master pianists. They were gentle when they needed to be, and forceful when they wanted to be. They were soft, and hard, and fast and slow. They were everything, and they were more. They were together, as Robins in the Night.

*"Ahem."*

And with a clear of a throat, the atmosphere of the room dissipated as quickly as it does when a cat is thrown into a room of mice. The Robins fluttered apart, and saw another in the doorway.

Celinda stood squarely, rooted, immovable, and they were terrified.

"So this is what you've been doing." Celinda said, not asked.

"Well, we…" Jemima began.

"There is, if you remember, a competition. A contest. A set of trials. To determine who gets to execute a man for stealing a loaf of bread. You two have stolen worse, and yet have never been faced with the threat of execution, which is, presumably, why you are able to sit here in comfort, lounging and chatting, while a dire situation draws nearer."

Marian began to speak, but Celinda raised a hand.

"Do you have a plan? Either of you? Are you simply hoping to enter a contest, win by some arbitrary stroke of luck, and then flee with the sword meant for the execution? Oh, or are you planning to steal the sword the night before? Because stealing the axe worked tremendously well didn't it, ladies?"

Jemima began to speak, but Celinda raised a hand more aggressively.

"Because of that incident, one of our own is dead, and one we ought to consider our own is still marked for execution. And here you are- master criminals. The only true crime you are committing is not facing reality."

Marian and Jemima both began to speak, but Celinda raised a hand quicker than her aged frame would lead one to believe was possible.

"You have baked a cake. You have actually baked a cake. That is something that you thought was a good idea. You saw cake ingredients- did you at least steal those? - and thought "oh, yes, well if we have the ingredients, we absolutely must bake a cake and then sit on our arses eating it"."

Marian and Jemima were silent, and both blushing, and made no attempt to speak.

"Let me ask you, ladies: Are you fucking serious, hm?"

Celinda folded her arms. Marian and Jemima exchanged glances, and then looked down solemnly at the plates of half-eaten slices of cake on their laps.

Never before had anybody looked so ashamed about cake.

# Intermission Two

Elsewhere, chess.

A white kingside pawn moved forward two spaces, and it saw a black kingside knight approach on the horizon, ending two spaces in front of a bishop.

Leonard Garden-Hand approached Priestess Trinna's well-lit house. Stood outside was Sir Patton Cross, talking to an unknown person wearing a green coat in the doorway.

A leftmost white pawn moved forward two spaces, and the aforementioned knight leapt forward to seize the white pawn.

Sir Patton Cross saw Leonard Garden-Hand approach. The unknown person wearing a green coat leapt over a fence and ran, practically flying like a robin into the night. Leonard briefly considered giving chase, but instead focused squarely on Patton.

A white queenside pawn moved one space forward, forcing the black knight to retreat backwards, securing its previous position in front of the bishop. A white rook moved to stand behind the leftmost pawn, and a black kingside pawn marched two spaces forwards.

"Do you think you'll win?" an old, dusty voice asked as a Mediterranean hand lingered on a pawn.

"Do you think you'll win?" a middle-aged, slightly bored voice asked as Priestess Trinna stepped out of her house, pushing past Patton Cross and attempting to bar both entry and exit with her arm.

## Chapter Twenty-One: A Viable Plan

Marian hurried to her kitchen and dumped the plates on the counter, vowing to clean them later. She told herself she would absolutely clean them later. She would not clean them later. More important things were happening.

Celinda stood in Marian's front room, staring down at Jemima who still sat on the couch, though she was leaning forward to put on her boots and tie the laces.

"You have not answered my question," Celinda said, monotone and serious, but Jemima still did not answer, "About whether you are serious."

Jemima looked up, having finished tying her shoelaces. They were tied haphazardly, hurriedly, and would probably fall loose after a maximum of forty-two steps. She met Celinda's intense gaze.

"Yes. We baked a cake." Jemima said, plainly, matter-of-factly, entirely truthfully. Inside, she felt like she could say infinitely more, like she could rant for hours about the interruption of her moment with Marian, but outwardly she stood, rigid, like a statue brought to life who does not quite know how to walk yet.

"Not about that, young lady." Celinda whispered, a sudden change in tone and pitch.

"Then what?" Jemima asked with a confused hand gesture.

"About *Marian. You and Marian. Are. You. Serious?*"

"What does serious mean in this context, Celinda?"

"Are you serious about each other? When you say that you are in love- that you love each other, when you see that it is suddenly not too soon for that."

Jemima's lip quivered. She wanted to look away from Celinda, but refused to let herself give in that easily. Celinda was the undisputed queen of unofficial staring contests but Jemima was next in line for the throne.

"Yes." She said, at last.

Celinda stood forward, looking deep into her eyes. She then looked down, forfeiting the staring contest but absorbing every detail of Jemima. The way she stood, her clenched fists hiding sweating palms, and then back to her eyes which had begun to water slightly, a minor overflow compared to the rain outside but a major deciding factor for Celinda.

"Yes. Yes, you are. That is correct. Thank you."

Marian re-entered the room.

"Now," Celinda began to command, "My coat is already waterlogged, so I have no quarrel with being back out in the rain. However, you two may want to cover up more warmly. After all, the rain is not as sweet as cake."

Celinda headed towards the front door. Jemima picked up her coat, and Marian started to pick up hers, but then stopped.

"Where are we going?" She asked.

"The same place we go every night, Marian. The tavern in the hidden corner of the world."

They stepped out of the house. At roughly the same time, Leonard Garden-Hand stepped into the guard barracks.

"You'll stay here," he said to Patton Cross, "As it's the only place we can keep a proper eye on you for the next few days."

Patton Cross made no response as he was pushed into a tiny cell in a back room. It was dingy, dank, discoloured, damp and dark in here. There was an odd smell that seemed to have no tangible source- it just stuck to the floor, walls and ceiling like invisible ink. It stuck to Patton as he stumbled in, colliding with the back wall as Leonard shoved him.

"You know, Cross," Leonard mused, "I didn't want to arrest you. It's not that I didn't think you ought to be brought to justice, you understand- it's that I didn't want to have to be the one to do it. I don't deem you worth the effort, sir, I have to be frank."

Patton turned, squinting at the silhouetted form of Leonard in the doorway.

"Because, you see, you're a criminal. That's why you're in here, do you know that? You stole, and you were to face justice. But that's not the end of it. The end of it is that after being given a second chance at life, you stole more. You stole even more than what you stole to get yourself executed. I don't understand that."

Leonard leaned against the door frame.

"Nobody would have stopped you if you'd just hopped aboard the next ship out of the country and left. We would've been glad, do you know? We would. Have been. Glad."

Patton folded his arms. Leonard folded his own in mockery.

"So now, we've got a contest to decide who gets to kill you! I won't be entering, though. Don't you worry. I don't want to kill you. I want you dead, naturally, but I don't want to be the one to have to kill you. Do you know why?"

Patton said nothing.

"It's because, sir, I don't deem people like you worth the effort."

He stood out of the doorway and slammed the door, barring it and securing the three locks from outside, before wandering off to the tower to see the Prince.

In the most basic of cells, Patton slumped against a wall, falling to a sitting position. He landed perfectly in a puddle of leaked rainwater.

Stepping over a puddle of rainwater, Celinda lead the two younger women into the forest.

"Ladies, dears, young women," She spoke almost to herself as she looked directly forward, unwavering in her goal, "We are concerned for you both. It seems you have leapt head-first into a decision and not thought of how you intend to achieve your ends."

She pushed a bramble away from her face.

"We should like to help you. All of us, at the tavern. And not just the Council..." She trailed off as she dodged a pond, "To form a viable plan."

Marian and Jemima looked at each other in uncertainty.

"What is your plan, thus far, my dear?" Celinda asked.

Marian stepped on a twig. It crunched and snapped under her foot, making a noise like thirty people snapping their fingers at once. It punctuated the silence preceding Marian's inability to reply.

"That is what I thought," Celinda sighed, brushing a fallen leaf off her shoulder, "And what I feared."

In silence, they continued their trek through the forest. Despite being under the cover of the leaves, the rain reached them in the harshest way possible, an impossible number of drops crashing against their heads as they walked the well-trodden and now awfully wet path through the woods.

"So," Jemima said out of a perceived necessity, "We're going to the tavern.... And we're going to make a plan?"

"And everybody's there?" Marian asked.

"Of course. We would like to help, as I say. We do not want to send you out there alone, hm? We are a council for a reason."

Rain fell on leaves, and leather boots crunched on stones and dry pieces of bark, and nobody said anything for a good ten seconds.

"I'm sorry about the cake." Marian said, but Celinda, to Marian's surprise, only laughed.

"That is probably the first time in history anyone has said that sentence," Celinda said between quiet laughs, "And it's okay, dear. It's not that I blame you for this situation. As I keep saying, we just want to help, and how am I supposed to react when I find you eating sweets at such a dangerous time?"

Marian laughed to herself. They had reached the old, rusted gate connected to the broken fence that ran off into the forest, into darker holes where usually the light of the moon could not reach but which were now exposed, the rain having forced the leaves to a position where moonlight could more successfully penetrate the canopy and illuminate the surroundings. To Marian, this was uncomfortable- she was used to leaves providing cover. It was a heavy factor in her fondness of the road she lived on. Even sometimes during the day the leaves provided enough shadow for her to sit and not be seen. But now, even this far away from the city, she felt the threat of danger in every raindrop slipping down her neck.

They arrived at the slope, the final part of the journey to the Golden Arrow. It was drenched, looking more like a muddy waterfall than anything else. Marian gulped as she looked at it. It did not seem safe at all.

Celinda sighed again and turned, walking left, in a completely separate direction. Jemima and Marian stood, mystified, watching Celinda walk away. Eventually the old woman turned and beckoned the two younger women with her arm.

"Come on," she implored, "You don't expect to go down that steep slope, surely? Come the other way around."

Jemima recoiled slightly in shock, "The *other* way around?"

Celinda raised her arms again in a gesture that said "Well, yes".

"Well, yes," Celinda said with her mouth, "Do you mean to tell me you didn't know?"

"Do you mean to tell me that for years now I've been slipping down that slope when there's a safer and easier way?"

"Of course there is! Look at me! My frame is about as sturdy as a snail's shell, and if I were to force myself up and down that slope every evening I would surely fall apart."

Jemima looked Celinda up and down, then turned and looked the slope up and down, then dropped her arms in resignation.

"Okay. The other way around."

Marian went along with it. The past few days she had been exposed to so many changes, new people and new dangers, that walking a longer way around to a tavern she had only visited a couple of times was nothing.

Jemima, however, seemed distraught. This was, to her, like she had been drinking from the same cup for a year and a half only for it to shatter into pieces one day and for her to be presented with a new cup that was a completely different size, shape, and colour, and expected to drink from it as if it was totally normal and this was the same cup she had always been using and nothing had changed or broken and everything was absolutely fine and any emotional response she had to the loss of her familiar cup was completely unjustified because, after all, it was just a cup.

Celinda seemed indifferent, and walked the path around the slope as though it were nothing. Naturally, she had walked this path many times before, and therefore it was, in essence, nothing to her. However, she had not walked it very many times under this particular amount of heavy rainfall, and after several steps in the direction she thought she knew well enough to travel in without thinking, she slipped, and almost fell.

Jemima leapt forward, demonstrating once more her almost-lightning reflexes, catching Celinda by her arm with one hand and reaching underneath her and catching her back with the other. Lifting Celinda up and getting her back on her feet, she panted, out of breath, as though she had been the one who fell.

"Are you alright? You weren't hurt? Everything's okay?" she asked in rapid staccato.

"Yes, yes, yes, let go," Celinda replied in a huff before raising a hand and smiling, "But you see why we must all work together to keep one another safe? We are not alone, hm?"

Patton Cross was alone, in his cell, which barely met the description of the word. He had no bed, no chair- he had nothing except the wet floor on which he sat. He had taken off his coat and draped it on the ground and stretched it as far as it would go, but it was not far. He wanted to lie down, to feel something below his aging back, but he dared not for fear of dampness seeping through his clothes.

There was a barred hole on the ceiling, through which the rain was falling. He almost wished a coincidentally located streak of lightning would pierce its way through the gaps between bars and strike him where he sat, but he did not hold out hope. He felt as though the clouds, as angry as they currently were, would probably not deem people like him worth the effort.

He wondered what Leonard had meant by "people like" him. He did not wonder for long. He wondered why he had bothered wondering. He knew what Leonard meant.

The guards here did not care for anyone who was not white.

The guards in a lot of places did not care for anyone who was not white.

As far as Patton had seen, no guards anywhere cared for anyone who was not white. Patton had seen a lot of places, a lot of guards, and not a lot of caring.

Even the King's Guard did not care especially for anyone who was not white. In his order, and his regiment, he had been the only black man amongst over forty white men, and everybody noticed. He knew everybody noticed, and he knew what they were thinking when they did. He grew accustomed to it, and said nothing, for fear of hostility. What aggravated him was when people pretended they did not notice. He thought back to a conversation he had had long ago.

"It must be hard, being part of the King's Guard."

"It can be. It's a weird place to be, for a black man."

"Oh, that doesn't matter, surely?"

"… It does. There's forty-one other men, and they are all white. I am the only black man there."

"Oh, but, in all truthfulness, I hadn't even noticed you were black!"

"… When you say truthfulness… Do you in fact know what that means?"

"What?"

"Of course you noticed I'm black. It's impossible to not notice I'm black. My face is black, my hair is black, all of my skin is black. You are white, and all of your friends are similarly white. It is absolutely not true that you did not notice that I am black, and in saying that you are simply saying that you choose to ignore situations of racial prejudice by pretending race isn't an issue. Which is entirely possible for you, as a white person, to do. But not for me. Being black is my life. I notice it every day."

The person he had been talking to fell quite silent at that moment. It was almost a shame, Patton had thought, because he had mentally prepared a second monologue that he could deploy if the argument continued. It was the second most aggravating silence of his life.

The absolute most aggravating silence was right now. This silence echoed around the empty room, bouncing off the walls like a rubber ball, knocking into the sides of Patton's head, causing a dull, throbbing headache that served as repeated full stops at the end of sentences formed by constant cascading rain.

Rain.

Rain.

Rain.

Rain.

"Hello?"

Rain.

Wait.

Patton looked up. There was somebody above the room, on the roof, leaning over the barred hole in the ceiling.

The trio of women slipped into the tavern. Some people turned and gave encouraging nods. Some people stood and gave encouraging handshakes. Some people did not acknowledge their presence, but took drinks that may or may not have been encouraging.

Deryn stood, a tower over the crowd like the stone monolith in the town square, in the doorway to the table room. She nodded, opened the door, and entered, all in silence while the tavern room grew noisier and noisier. Marian, Jemima and Celinda all followed her, and took their seats at the table, surrounded by all their fellow members of the Council except Aleta.

They began to talk, and discuss, and plot, together. They focused, and combined their thoughts. They made a viable plan.

In Patton's cell, the figure on the roof spoke to him. It was not who he had expected.

He had not expected any visitors. He had expected, if he was to somehow get visitors despite how unlikely it seemed to be, for those visitors to be any of several people, but not this person was not on this list at all.

It was not that he did not know this bizarre visitor- he did, in fact, know this person, but only vaguely. They had met once, but Patton was not well acquainted with them.

Really, technically and logically, it can be extremely difficult to be acquainted with a person in the same line of work as the person who was on the cell roof.

Meeting this kind of person does not usually result in the possibility of a second conversation. Not many people at all have much of a chance to talk to them for very long even during one conversation.

Generally, one would see this type of person at the end of the day, or at the end of a week, or a month, or a life, and would not see them, or anyone else, again. This is why this situation was unusual.

Patton wondered if this was some sort of sickening metaphor.

"Hello?" said the voice again, and Patton's theory of metaphor was disproven entirely. It was not a metaphor. It was as literal as a situation can get.

The executioner was crouched on Patton's roof, staring down at him through the barred hole.

## Chapter Twenty-Two: The Day in Question

Some time passed, as it always does. Time is never not passing, especially in the city of early risers.

A woman left an old man with his house and his rock cakes and his chessboard intact, but his dignity crushed like an insurmountable dream, his winning streak taken from him mercilessly as though he were a meagre pawn against a queen.

A man swore he could feel himself rotting in a cell, his sole visitor having left him behind entirely. He was starving now, and another man lingered outside his cell, a key hovering in front of the lock- not scared to make the leap, but savouring the moments that built up to it.

Two men on a boat arrived in a port town across a short stretch of the ocean. They had left behind all they held dear, and all they had never wanted to admit they hated.

A woman awoke in her house and gathered papers for a sermon she wished she did not have to perform.

A man awoke in his bed and laughed uproariously and victoriously at an empty picture frame.

Two women awoke in a bed made primarily of pillows. They did not speak, for they did not need to.

It was the day of the contest, and the city was almost literally aflame. The sun was beating down angrily in a cloudless sky, presumably its revenge against the storm of the past few nights.

On days like today, huge events, the people wore red. It was a tradition handed down through the centuries from the original founders of the city, whose names and genders had been lost to time, though their traditions had not. Red was their ceremonial colour. Almost all of the citizens, therefore, wore some piece of red clothing. A baker wearing an old red apron sold a loaf of bread to a woman wearing a vibrant red scarf. This woman proceeded to a butcher wearing a red shirt. She bought red meat, and took it home. Her children ran to the door- two girls, in matching red dresses. They would be the fanciest children at the contest, or she would be damned.

The bustle of the city- everybody dashing about, hurried conversations and a never ending shuffle of feet- combined with all of their red clothing made the city appear to be ablaze. From above, in a room at the top of a tower, it would appear to any onlookers as if a tiny spark somewhere had ignited some hitherto unseen flammable substance and coated absolutely everything it could reach in crimson.

The Prince in the room he had officially claimed as his own atop the tower went all out on the redness of the day. He wore an outfit entirely in different shades of red- a shirt, trousers, formal shoes, leather gloves, and a cape, as he had heard that all the most destructive princes wear capes.

His pointed beard was already ginger but frankly, he thought, that wasn't red enough. He had a servant wake up even earlier than they normally would to cut up some beetroot, and boil it, and go through many more steps of an arduous process that produced a bowl of red dye. The servant, exhausted, carried this bowl into the Prince's room and presented it to him in simultaneous revulsion and reverence. The Prince laughed once more and slathered the beet juice dye all over his chin and neck.

When he was done, he had the reddest beard imaginable. He looked, in summation, like an oversized and unnecessarily muscular tomato, and smelled heavily of beetroot. For good measure he slapped some remaining beet juice under his armpits, to "freshen his scent", as he put it, and to "enhance his manly stature", as he secondly put it, and to "be a total assault on everybody's senses", as a servant thirdly put it under their breath as they left the room.

All the servants were of course also wearing red. They had special uniforms in their communal wardrobe for just such occasions, that were identical to their regular uniforms but in deep scarlet. As they had changed into these uniforms earlier in the day, one servant commented that they had found a uniform outside, in the yard, just lying around, completely soaked through. None of the other servants knew how that had happened.

Whilst in the yard, the servant had picked up the golden sword, and had noted that it was not actually made of gold. It was painted to look that way, and sharpened as sharp as a sword can be sharpened, but it was not gold. The servant thought this was especially cheap considering apparently this was the kind of establishment that burned priceless, ancient paintings by esteemed rulers who were much fairer and kinder than the current authorities. The servant said none of this out loud. The servant would not dare. The servant was, after all, a servant.

They carried the sword to the guard barracks, where it would be inspected and kept by Leonard Garden-Hand, the Chief of the Guard.

Leonard Garden-Hand, the Chief of the Guard, was currently stood outside the room containing Sir Patton Cross. He had inspected the sword, noted its shimmer and the obsequious pandering of the servant, and approved it. It would be a fine prize for the winner of the contest, he thought.

Then, he laughed.

Then, he laughed even more.

Then, he laughed so much that he forgot to let Patton Cross out of his cell.

Patton Cross listened to the Chief laugh outside and stood up, intending to bang on the door, but lost his balance in a light-headed daze and slipped to the ground, falling immediately unconscious as Leonard took a leisurely stroll across the town square which already bustled with excitement.

Also in the town square, Marian and Jemima leaned against a building. They held hands, out of necessity, and to show solidarity.

Today, their solidarity meant love. They did not know if or when they would get a chance to love each other again, and so they showed it through their hands now.

The town crier stepped out of the tower, and the crowd turned to face him. All was hushed, and he began to roar the words that would define the path of the rest of Marian's life.

"HEAR YE ALL," He said, reading from a scroll, "THE CONTEST WILL BEGIN IN HALF AN HOUR. THERE ARE A TOTAL OF THREE CONTESTANTS."

Jemima squeezed Marian's hand reassuringly.

"THE FIRST, OUR BELOVED PRINCE AND SHERIFF, *WILLIAM ALAN ANCHOR.*"

The King's brother stepped out of the tower, raising his arms proudly, wafting the smell of beetroot around a cloud that clapped politely.

"THE SECOND, A COMMONER… A LADY BY THE NAME OF *OLIVIA CULTO.*"

A woman with all of her face but her eyes covered who matched exactly the height and weight of Aleta suddenly appeared from the crowd closest to the town crier. She bowed low, and then stood again, and whispered in the crier's ear.

"… WHO I AM INFORMED," continued the crier, "HAS HER FACE COVERED FOR RELIGIOUS REASONS… AND ANYBODY WHO WANTS TO SAY SOMETHING ABOUT IT CAN TRY TO SAY IT TO HER FACE BUT IS GUARANTEED TO BE UNSUCCESSFUL FOR REASONS THAT OUGHT TO BE OBVIOUS."

"Is that…?" Marian asked.

"It is. It definitely is." Jemima replied.

Aleta, better known as Olivia Culto now, bowed again and returned to the crowd, who gave a tiny smattering of slightly concerned applause.

"AND OUR THIRD AND FINAL CONTESTANT,"

Marian's palms began to sweat.

"IN OUR LITTLE TOURNAMENT TO WIN THE GOLDEN SWORD,"

Marian's heart raced, as it had done so much recently.

"WITH WHICH WILL COME THE RIGHT TO EXECUTE KNOWN CRIMINAL PATTON CROSS,"

Marian's throat felt entirely dry.

"IS ANOTHER COMMONER,"

Marian's head felt light.

"BY THE NAME,"

Marian's legs began to shake.

"OF *MARIAN STOKE*."

Marian entered writer mode. She was acclaimed author, writer, wordsmith, and ink and paper artist, Marian Stoke. She would own this moment in spite of the terror that filled her entire being, flowing through her veins like rain trickling down a cobblestone road. She stepped forward, raising her right arm, her palm open wide for all to see.

The crowd gave the same smattering of applause they had given Aleta. It was good enough for Marian. She did not care much for uproarious applause. It always seemed artificial, and insincere, and even if it were all truthful and real she did not feel like she deserved it.

The town crier cleared his throat. The town crier's throat needed clearing a lot, as is a common requirement of throats that are used almost constantly.

"THE CONTEST WILL TAKE PLACE IN WYNN PARK," he said, "TO THE EAST OF THE SQUARE. MAKE YOUR WAY THERE NOW FOR THE BEST VIEW OF THE CONTEST. I WILL SEE YOU ALL THERE." The town crier smiled with the satisfaction of a job well done. He silently congratulated himself, and his throat, and began to make his way with the rest of the crowd to the park on the opposite side of town to the graveyard.

"Did you know it was called Wynn Park?" Jemima asked awkwardly.

"Jemima- you don't have to distract me," Marian replied as affectionately as possible, "Now's the time for me to face reality, and hopefully everything will go to plan."

"But we don't know exactly how Aleta's plan is going to…"

"That's fine. Aleta's good at this. We'll work it out as long as we stick to the viable plan we made with everyone else."

Jemima blinked at the ground, her lips curling into a frown.

"… What's wrong?" Marian asked.

"… Nothing, yet. It's more the chance of something going wrong, or becoming wrong."

"Jemima."

"Marian?"

"I won't lie to you. There's a massive possibility that all of this could go wrong. I could get hurt, I could get jailed, I could get… Lots of things could happen. But we have to believe in ourselves and tell ourselves that we can do this. If we can convince ourselves, we can convince the rest of the world." Marian said, taking both of Jemima's hands.

Jemima smiled with wet eyes.

"You're right. I love you."

"I love you too. Let's go."

They walked in silence amongst the loud hubbub of the crowd, and when they arrived, they separated so that Marian could reach the front. The contest began.

Marian tried to focus on her breathing.

## Chapter Twenty-Three: Trials

In the park, a path of hot coals had been set up. Marian had no idea how they were transported here, and was afraid to speak to ask. There were so many people watching. It was the situation in the tavern from a few nights ago but much worse, and she could not pretend to be a popular and charismatic writer here. She stood alone, unable to see any familiar faces in the crowd, under the relentless sunlight.

"THE TRIAL BY FIRE WILL NOW BEGIN," shouted the town crier, "AND ITS GOAL WILL BE THUS: WHOMEVER CAN CROSS THE RIVER OF COALS MOST QUICKLY WILL BE THE VICTOR."

With all the citizens stood around in red, looking for all the world like an inferno made of humans, the contestants stepped forward.

Marian's heart pounded incessantly. She was grateful that it was reminding her of its presence, but rather wished it would calm down.

Aleta's palms began to sweat, and she loved it. The atmosphere welled within her like a warm drink on a cold night.

The Prince scowled at the world in general, and stepped forward once more.

"I will go first." He stated, his voice exerting more pressure than a dropped anvil, and the trial by fire began. The coals glowed brightly in front of him, but he barely looked at them as he took off his shoes. The whole crowd stared, enraptured, as he tossed the shoes aside, wiggled his monstrous toes and, for the third time, stepped forward.

He stepped onto the coals and walked casually over them. With every step, the crowd took sharp breaths, anticipating his screams of agony, but they did not come. He reached the other side without incident.

The crowd cheered.

Aleta stepped forward during the commotion and leaned over to unlace her boots. Before anybody had much of a chance to react, she skipped delicately over the coals, barely making any contact with them at all, dancing over the danger as though it were nothing. The crowd cheered even louder, and the Prince briefly considered pushing Aleta into the coals for stealing his thunder.

It was Marian's turn.

It felt like an eternity as she walked forward, striding deliberately over the coals. She felt like she was operating outside of reality, for a moment, like she was watching herself walk over the coals from some vantage point high above her. She was snapped back into reality just as she reached the other side, unscathed, and the crowd cheered louder than ever before. The town crier rang his bell.

"THE TRIAL BY FIRE IS DONE," he bellowed, "AND THE WINNER WILL BE DECIDED BASED ON SPEED."

The crowd and the three contestants listened on tenterhooks as the crier turned to the jury. They all seemed to reach the same conclusion, and the crier cleared his throat.

"THE WINNER OF THE TRIAL BY FIRE IS… *OLIVIA CULTO.*" He declared, gesturing with one arm to Aleta, who may have smiled under her facial cover, but nobody could be certain.

The Prince folded his arms in a huff.

"THE FIRST TRIAL BY COMBAT WILL NOW COMMENCE. WHOMEVER CAN BRING DOWN THEIR OPPONENT QUICKEST WILL BE THE VICTOR."

Three large men stepped out of the crowd. Or rather, they pushed and shoved so that the crowd stepped out of their way. They were made of similar proportions to the executioner, but were all shirtless.

Marian was slightly distracted by their muscles for a moment. They were the most defined muscles she had ever seen. It was interesting.

She shook off these thoughts and refocused on her real goal: to take her opponent down.

The three contestants stood at equidistant intervals apart in an open plane of the field. Their opponents lined up before them, and silence swept over the crowd like a wave washing over a secluded shore.

"THREE... TWO... ONE... BEGIN." The town crier commanded, and the first trial of combat began.

The Prince pointed his large opponent in the face, then gestured to the floor. His opponent fell on command, and the Prince smiled smugly. Marian and Aleta both turned, confused, unsure whether they ought to continue. The two opponents who remained standing were equally perplexed, and looked at each other for reassurance that they weren't imagining things.

They were not imagining things. The Prince had definitely just won this round.

"THE... WINNER IS PRINCE WILLIAM ALAN ANCHOR?" The town crier questioned more than stated.

"You're damn fucking right the winner is Prince William Alan Anchor." The Prince responded, as self-satisfied as the sun was bright.

The town crier approached the jury again and asked what to do. They mumbled angrily, all hisses and dissonant whispers. The town crier gestured with his arms as if to say "well it isn't MY fault" and then turned back.

"THE... SECOND TRIAL OF COMBAT. THIS IS WHERE ONE OF YOU WILL BE ELIMINATED FROM THE PROCEEDINGS. EACH OF YOU WILL FIGHT THE SAME OPPONENT. YOUR GOAL WILL BE TO FELL THEM... BUT THE FIRST ONE OF YOU TO FALL WILL BE DISQUALIFIED FROM THE CONTEST. YOU MAY BEGIN AS SOON AS YOUR OPPONENT IS READY."

Leather boots crunched and stomped on the grass of the park. Their opponent approached.

He was seven feet tall, and built sturdier than the Earth he walked on. His beard covered his neck and his arms bulged with muscle that was almost painful to look at as it stretched the fabric of his shirt. The entire crowd fell silent out of a mixture of fear and quiet excitement.

The headsman, the executioner, the axe wielder. Their opponent. He had arrived.

The Prince, as usual, went first. He readied his fists. The executioner also readied his fists. Their fists were both as readied as fists can possibly be. Their chests were both cavernous, all four forearms they held between the two of them were like tree trunks, and they both had looks in their eyes that, if they were to be transcribed into words, would spell out "You stand no chance. I am going to beat you down".

A fist flew, and was blocked. Another fist flew, and was blocked. A fist collided with a stomach, and then again, and a third time.

The executioner fell to his knees. The Prince had won. He flung his arms up in victory and marched off to a satisfactory point at which to watch the further fights.

Aleta, or Olivia, approached the executioner as he stood himself back up again. They held eye contact for what seemed like much longer than they should have. Aleta raised a hand. The executioner simply pushed her aside. She fell, and was disqualified.

*What?* Marian thought. *Is this on purpose?*

She did not have time to think much further into this. It was her turn. She stepped forward.

*Fuck.* She thought.

*FUCK.* She thought, beginning to panic.

*HE'S FUCKING HUGE.* She thought at last as the cheering of the crowd died out and it became time for her to face the music. If "music" meant "seven foot hulking slab of muscle and meat".

He stood in front of her. He was at least a foot taller than her. She felt like a regular building in the town square standing in front of the huge stone tower.

He continued to stand in front of her. He didn't move. She didn't know why he didn't move.

She just wanted to get this over with. She took a step forward, and he took a step forward too. They were close together now, in silence apart from his grunting breaths.

He stepped even closer. She was terrified but followed suit, standing mere inches from the headsman now.

It wasn't long ago that she was stealing his axe, and that had been scary enough. But now, to face him directly, was even worse. She had preferred him being a nameless threat.

Quite suddenly, the town crier cleared his throat.

"TECHNICALLY THERE IS NO REASON FOR THIS TO BE GOING ON AS WE ALREADY HAVE A CONTESTANT DISQUALIFIED..." He said, but trailed off as Marian had jumped in surprise at the interruption and hit the executioner lightly with the back of her hand.

The executioner fell.

Marian watched him fall backwards, landing with a crash on the grass.

"I... Hello? Headsman?" She whispered, tentatively leaning over, "I didn't... I didn't hit you that hard? What are you doing?"

The town crier once more interrupted.

"THE TRIALS OF COMBAT ARE OVER. ONTO THE NEXT TRIAL! PRINCE WILLIAM ALAN ANCHOR AND MARIAN STOKE WILL BE COMPETING IN THE TRIAL OF ARCHERY IN HALF AN HOUR."

The crowd dispersed to seek some form of food or drink in this interval. The Prince went with them, as did the town crier. Jemima ran to Marian's side as she stood staring at the executioner who was slowly standing up.

"Marian- do you need a drink?" Jemima panted, worn out just from watching.

"No. No, I need to know why this man fell from the slightest hit." Marian replied, forcefully, but not overly harshly.

Jemima grabbed Marian's arm.

"Just leave it, please," she said, "It doesn't matter, the round's over now."

The executioner was now at his full height again. He grunted.

"Hello." He said.

"Hello?" Marian asked.

"If the Prince wins the contest, he will kill Patton Cross."

"… Yes? Which is what you were going to do several days ago anyway."

The executioner shifted uncomfortably.

"I'm sorry. I don't want to hurt people."

Jemima and Marian exchanged glances.

"Then why are you an executioner?" Jemima asked.

"What else is there?" he said, mumbling at the ground.

Marian furrowed her brow, and Jemima cocked her head slightly to the side.

"I talked to Patton. Patton stole bread, and Patton will be executed? It isn't right. I don't want to be an executioner any more if people will die for… For nothing. I… Want to help. So I let you win."

"But the town crier said we didn't have to fight, technically."

"But the Prince would have made us. Now, you are further in the competition. And Olivia… Aleta."

Jemima and Marian looked at each other, concerned.

"Aleta… Slipped away. She will be causing a distraction, she said. So you…"

"Marian, we can steal the sword." Jemima whispered. Marian nodded.

"Thank you… Executioner." Marian said, offering her hand to shake it. The executioner slowly raised his huge fist and took Marian's hand with the most surprisingly gentle touch Marian had ever experienced.

"I am not an executioner. My name is Bob Grunt."

Marian thought for a moment.

"That's a lovely name, Bob Grunt. Just wondering, though. Would you like your axe back?"

Bob Grunt shook his head violently.

"No."

Bob Grunt paused for a moment, confused.

"You stole it?"

Marian nodded.

"Well done." Said Bob Grunt. With that, he smiled, and he turned, and he walked away. The executioner left.

But this was not a time for heartfelt goodbyes. This was a time for sword stealing. The two women quickly exited the park, discussing the plan as they went. They would rely on the distraction from Aleta- or Olivia, if that was what she wanted to be called- in order to sneak into the guard barracks and retrieve the sword. All the guards would be out at the front of the building, protecting against the general swarming that would be the town square in the half hour before the next contest trial. All they would have to do would be to sneak in the back door.

However, the door was not literal. To get in, they would actually have to climb up on the roof of the stone annex built out of the back of the building, wrench away the bars on the ceiling window, pick the lock from the inside, retrieve the sword and go back out the way they came.

They arrived back near the town square. Jemima stayed at the entrance to the back alley and watched for Aleta's distraction while Marian lurked in the shadows beside her.

Aleta, with her face still covered, emerged from the crowd, holding a brick. She threw it at the fountain, and it collided with an ear-splitting cracking noise. Everybody was suddenly facing her, as she opened a bag on her back and pulled out another. A guard shouted to another guard, who shouted to a third, who shouted to several more, and they began to run at her like schoolchildren rushing to see a fight on the other end of the playground.

Marian took this opportunity to slide further into the shadows and begin to make her way around the back of the guard barracks.

Jemima watched as the guards chased Aleta away.

Jemima also watched as Leonard Garden-Hand, the Chief of the Guard, turned squarely to the guard barracks and marched directly towards them.

Before Jemima could warn Marian, she was already gone. She had climbed onto the roof of the stone annex behind the barracks and stomped heavily down on the bars of the window, causing them to fall inwards and clatter on the floor. She dropped in, gripping the edge of the hole with bare hands, and landing on her feet on the wet floor within.

Patton Cross looked up, blearily. Marian crouched down for a moment, checking he was alright. Before she could offer him some food from her pockets or stand up to pick the lock on the door, Leonard Garden-Hand opened it from the outside.

He stood in the doorway staring down at Marian.

"Well, well, well," He said, "What have we here?"

# Chapter Twenty-Four: The Fall

There was a basement in the guard barracks that functioned as a tunnel underneath the town square to the basement of the stone tower. Marian was surprised to see it, but upon reflection, it made sense. Sometimes nobles would need an escape. But now, she was not escaping. She was being lead into the tower.

Leonard forced her into a room, tied her to a chair and locked the door.

Marian sat alone for what felt like the first time in years.

It was an odd sensation now, being alone. To not be in Jemima's company. She'd been lonely plenty of times, but it felt as though she had never been alone before. She remembered long nights spent alone before she met Jemima, when nobody had slept next to her and when she could always be certain that she would not wake up in somebody's arms. She remembered the past few nights, sleeping with Jemima in every sense of the term, and it was odd, because just a few recent nights made all the loneliness in the world feel miles away and years ago.

She wanted to explain this baffling feeling to Jemima, because she'd understand. But now, even though there were other people in the tower, she was alone. Truly alone.

Fear struck through her, crashing down on her chest like a clenched fist on an unsuspecting snail when she thought of Jemima and of Aleta, and the rest of the Council. Where were they now? Were they even alive? Were they trying to find her? If they were looking, could they even hope to find her? The tower was tall, and well-guarded, and she wasn't sure anybody apart from the guards themselves knew the basement existed.

How would they know where to look?

Nothing could be sure now except what was around her. The basement was basic, and met the minimum standards of the concept of humane. Her bed was soft, but the linen was old. There was a picture frame hung on the wall by the door, but no picture in the frame. She thought perhaps her captors just appreciated fine frames and had no need for pictures. She continued to wonder what sort of people appreciate "fine frames". She smiled at how silly this idea was. She imagined walking into an old museum expecting to see tapestries and paintings of ancient rulers and famous battles and there just being empty frames with people stood around making approving noises. She started to laugh to herself as she imagined a stuffy, dusty old man giving a lecture on the history of picture frames.

Maybe, she thought, this was the point of the frame. Maybe it's a sort of statement, maybe the lack of any art in the frame is so you make your own art in your head, maybe it's meant to say that as long as you know an arbitrarily decided space on the wall is where art is supposed to be, it doesn't matter what's in the space because your head automatically thinks "art".

She thought for a moment this was quite clever, and then realised it was exactly what pretentious nobles visiting the tower would say. She imagined them in the Halls of Empty Picture Frames again and the fit of giggles returned. She was still laughing when the door opened.

"Well it's good to see you're laughing, criminal scum." Leonard Garden-Hand said, walking behind her and pulling her wrist ties even tighter.

"Scum's a bit excessive." Marian sighed.

"Shut it." Leonard replied.

There was a pounding on the door that sounded as though it were being hit with a sack of potatoes.

"IS *IT* IN THERE?" The Prince's voice boomed from outside.

Leonard opened the door and let the Prince in. He stormed over to Marian and grabbed her by her hair.

"Oh absolutely shitting fuck. It's THIS one?"

"I'll leave you two alone…" Said Leonard, leaving the two of them alone.

"Hello, shit stain," The Prince began, "I can't help but notice you're a waste of fucking space. That's fun. Tell me about it."

Marian remained silent.

"Tell me how it feels to be a waste of fucking space."

Marian smiled at the Prince.

"TELL ME. HOW IT FEELS. YOU FUCKING *WASTE*."

"Feels good," Marian said as calmly as her nerves would allow, "Feels really, really good."

The Prince slapped her.

"It's been you, hasn't it? The whole fucking time? You ruined my day with the axe, and now you're back again trying to ruin my day with the sword? You fuck- shitting ball bag."

The Prince began to pace around the room.

"That Olivia woman won the first contest… And then I won the second… And oh, I won the third one too, but Olivia's gone. Looks like I'm in the lead. So d'you know what I'm going to do?"

The Prince stroked his beard.

"I'm going to have you killed. You've ruined my fucking fun all too often, you little bitch. I'm going to make sure your head's on the chopping block."

The Prince crouched in front of Marian.

"We knew you'd come, you know. We knew! We fucking knew. We knew you wouldn't be able to resist. Because you're filthy. You can't resist stealing. You fucking bit of pond weed. So we set this all up to lure you back. That was the plan. To get you arrested. And you played right into our fucking hands didn't you, you sack of worms?"

"So you're going to *execute* me?" Marian gasped, wrenching forward but being pulled back sharply by her wrist ties, "You're literally going to execute me for stealing. For *stealing*? I can just give it back."

"SHUT UP," roared the Prince, as Marian squinted in disgust, "YOU DISGUSTING PIECE OF BLACK FILTH."

"*Black filth?*"

"YOU HEARD ME. I SAID YOU'RE *BLACK FILTH.*"

"*BLACK* filth?"

The Prince swung around his arm as though it were a heavy wooden club and smacked the side of Marian's head.

"*BLACK. FILTH.*"

Marian, though her vision was blurred, still managed to speak.

"If I was white... Would you execute me?"

The Prince stood back, and looked Marian up and down. He took in every inch of her, absorbing every detail- lingering for longer than could ever have been necessary on her naturally tightly curled hair, and then lingering for even longer on her groin. He reached up a hesitant hand for a minute, resting it on her leg, and huffing. He stepped forward again, leaned down and squatted in front of the chair, looked Marian right in the eyes, turned his head diagonally to the left at an almost unnatural angle and grinned widely.

"What do you think, you filthy little man?" he asked in a voice barely above a whisper.

Marian's eyes widened, and though she was seeing double, she kept her gaze steadfast and strong for as long as possible.

"I'm not a man."

The Prince grabbed her face by her chin.

"You're a man."

"No," Marian stated firmly, "I'm absolutely not."

The Prince squeezed her cheeks, forcing her lips into an exaggerated pout.

"You've got balls," he whispered, "I can see their outline. So you're a man."

Marian was silent for a moment, waiting for her vision to clear. She saw the Prince close up in all of his greasy glory, and quickly lurched up her left leg and kicked the Prince in the groin with her thigh. The Prince let go of her face, and fell sideways, clutching himself and groaning.

"What the FUCK?" he cried.

"Balls don't define you as a man," said Marian, watching the Prince writhe in pain on the hard, cold stone floor, "If they do, I think your *manhood* just retreated inside your body."

Marian flung her arms sideways as hard and fast as possible, breaking the shoddily executed ties that bound her to the chair. She stood up, stepped over the belittled king's brother, opened the door and began to step out.

She stopped for a moment, and turned, watching the king's brother reach out for her from the ground in a futile attempt to stop her leaving.

"I'm a woman, you bigoted river of sludge. Go and do some soul searching."

She ran from the basement of the tower to the basement of the guard barracks, sprinted up the stairs two at a time, and entered a room with Leonard's name engraved on the door.

And there it was. The golden sword. Hers.

At that moment, Priestess Trinna burst into the guard barracks too. A guard tried to pull her away by her arm, but she slid out of the jacket she was wearing to escape his grip. She streamed straight to the stone annex room, unlocked the door with the keys still in the lock, dragged up Patton Cross and lead him out with an arm over his shoulder, kicking the guard that tried to stop her in the shin.

"Fair enough." The guard said, falling over.

As she left the barracks, Marian left Leonard's room, golden sword in hand. She walked out, ignoring the guard on the floor, and faced the bustling square once more. Some people turned to face her, and then rapidly backed away in terror. Near the fountain, the town crier was inspecting a bow and arrow. Jemima was nowhere to be seen, and the guards had chased Aleta away. Marian approached the centre of town and climbed up the side of the fountain as everybody looked on in shock, or confusion, or terror, or anything similar. The town crier gripped tightly to his bow.

Marian entered writer mode.

"Are you all happy?" She asked the world at large, "Are you all sure you're happy? This is a town, or a city, where people will be executed for petty theft. This is a country where contests will be held to decide who gets to execute them. This is a world where anyone who isn't white is described as literal filth, and transgender women are described as men. This is a time when all of us have to ask ourselves if we are happy, and if we are, we have to question *why*."

She held the golden sword high in the air.

"This," She continued, "Is the sword. The sword that has been promised to whoever wins the contest. A shoddily thought-out contest by all definitions- what is the point of the first two trials if somebody gets disqualified in the third? And *chess? Really?* Could you sincerely not think of anything, but you wanted five for whatever arbitrary reason you've come up with today?"

She moved the sword closer to the fountain.

"A sword of solid gold to the person who can beat the Prince at chess. Do you know something, too? This isn't solid gold. This is fucking paint."

She held the sword under the running water of the fountain, and indeed, the paint began to wash away, leaving cold, hard steel as all that remained. It caught the sun's rays and shined in people's eyes, a stark reality shaped like a blade.

"This is what they do. They paint things as though they're amazing, and act like we're lucky. And we all love it, because we're supposed to love it. We're supposed to love performing hard labour for people in stone towers, being given a tiny fraction of coin, and then giving it immediately back to the people in the stone towers."

She lowered the sword down by her side, but held on tightly.

"They execute us for thievery, but the real thieves? They're up there."

Marian turned and pointed up to the tower window.

Leonard Garden-Hand was leaning out of it, holding Jemima. He pushed.

She fell.

Time seemed to slow down as Marian watched Jemima fall. She half expected her to take flight and soar away, but she did not. She fell, closer and closer to the hard stone of the ground.

Marian dared not blink for fear that she would miss the moment. She wanted to miss no more moments. Every moment that Jemima was in her sight was absolutely precious now more than ever.

Her heart began to sink as Jemima's descent quickened.

Suddenly, there was change.

Suddenly, there was hope.

Suddenly, there was life.

Celinda, Deryn, Quilla, and Paloma all stepped out of the tower main door, holding a large green life net, one of them at each corner. They hurried into position, stretching it as far as it would go.

Jemima landed on it.

She was alive. Perfectly alive. She made eye contact with Marian, and smiled in relief, but then her smile turned into a look of confusion as she looked beyond Marian.

Xiang was striding across the town square. She pulled the bow and arrows away from the town crier and aimed upwards, diagonally.

"Push an unarmed girl out a window, will you? Organise a series of unfair trials, will you? Well then. Here's your trial by fucking archery." She said with the falsest cheeriness that has ever been mustered, and she let loose an arrow.

It flew straight and true and sunk itself into Leonard Garden-Hand's chest. He staggered backwards, clutching at the arrow, blood spilling over his hands. He collapsed onto the floor of the room at the top of the tower.

Xiang turned to the crowd.

"Justified?" She asked.

The crowd of citizens cheered. Even some guards cheered. The town crier raised his hands in a tiny, private celebration that he didn't quite want people to see.

Their celebrations were cut short, however, as another figure emerged from the tower, pushing its way past the women stood around the entrance.

The Prince had arrived. He pointed at Marian.

"CHESS." He exclaimed.

"A TRIAL BY CHESS." He roared.

"OR I'LL FUCKING BEAT THE SHIT OUT OF YOU." He finished as he walked towards her with a limp. Marian stepped forward to greet him, still wielding the sword.

"If you've got the board, I'll play with you."

"SERVANT." The Prince called, not breaking eye contact with Marian. A servant ran out of the tower holding a chess board, while another ran out with a small round table. A third ran out holding two chairs, one under each arm. They set them up in the square, and quickly set up the chess pieces. The Prince sat down, legs wide apart. Marian sat down, the sword at her side.

"I've been practicing," The Prince whispered to Marian, "With Leonard. So you're going the fuck down."

"I think Leonard is probably dead by now." Marian responded, much to the confusion of the Prince.

As usual, the Prince played white.

The Prince moved the pawn in front of his right bishop one space forward.

Marian moved her kingside pawn two spaces forward.

The Prince moved the pawn in front of his right knight forward two spaces.

Marian moved her queen diagonally, landing next to the second pawn the Prince had moved.

"Checkmate." Marian said.

"... OH FOR FUCK'S SAKE NOT AGAIN." The Prince roared, knocking over all of the pieces, scattering them over the ground, and grabbing Marian by her hair. Jemima started forward, but the Prince knocked her back with a swing of his arm.

"NEW PUNISHMENT FOR THIEVES," he exclaimed, pulling the sword from Marian's grip, "THEY LOSE THEIR FUCKING HAND."

He laid Marian's hand out on the table, and raised the sword to cut it off.

Jemima ran forward again, but was knocked back with one blow from his elbow.

Paloma and Quilla ran at once, and were both knocked back with a swing of his arm.

Xiang let loose another arrow. He caught it in his fist, and crushed it in his palm. Celinda threw the life net at him, but he slashed through it completely with the sword.

Marian began to resign herself to this fate. There was nothing that could be done.

"HEY, BEETROOT," came a voice from over by the tower, "OVER HERE."

It was Deryn's voice. She shouted loud enough for her words to echo off all the walls of the square, and the Prince lost his concentration, turning to face her.

Then, Aleta ran through the crowd, still pursued by guards. She leapt up, and grabbed the sword from his hand, pulling it away and continuing to run. A guard grabbed her shoulder, and then pulled at the facial cover, revealing her identity to all of those around her.

"*Aleta?*" Celinda whispered.

The Prince let go of Marian and stormed over to Aleta, attempting to pull the sword away from her. Aleta looked beyond and behind the Prince, and threw the sword over his shoulder.

Behind him stood Patton Cross. He caught the sword by its hilt and swung it into a fighting position.

"Touch a single hair on the head of any of these people and I will end you." Sir Patton Cross, esteemed knight of the King's Guard, specified.

The Prince stepped forward, enraged.

Patton swung the sword at him, and he screamed in agony and fell.

"Like you said," Patton said, "Thieves lose a hand."

The Prince was bleeding from his wrist, his blood staining the ground. The crowd all stepped back.

Prince William Alan Anchor roared, and stood once more, lurching towards Sir Patton Cross. With his one remaining hand, he wrenched the sword from Patton and ran it through his stomach.

He pulled the sword out and held it aloft.

"AND WITH THAT," he bellowed, "THE CRIMINAL IS DEAD, AND THE SPECTACLE IS OVER. SERVANTS. BANDAGE MY FUCKING STUMP WRIST."

Nobody moved.

"SERVANTS."

Still, nobody moved.

"BANDAGE."

Everybody stayed exactly where they were.

"WHAT... What are you doing?" his voice seemed to rise three octaves as it dropped in volume.

"Why aren't you bandaging... Why? That's... A lot of blood."

He began to sway, and tip from side to side. The sword clattered at his feet.

"Was it something I said?"

The king's brother stumbled and fell over the chess table, his head on the board, in a daze caused by blood loss.

Priestess Trinna stepped forwards from the crowd, picked up the sword from the floor, brought it over her head, and slammed it down on the king's brother's neck. His head toppled off the chess board onto the floor with a dull thud, like a full stop at the end of a sentence.

She turned to the crowd.

"*Justified?*" she asked.

The crowd cheered.

## Chapter Twenty-Five: Robins in the Day

The oppressive rule of the king's brother had ended, officially. But it was not all.

Patton Cross had lost his life. It had seemed for all the world as though he would survive, but it was simply not to be. The best nurses and doctors in the town could not bandage the wound left by the sword. Priestess Trinna mourned him dearly, like a brother. She had presided over his funeral, and it was a frankly harrowing experience.

But in terms of siblings, she had also gained one.

She had reunited with her younger sister, and her Aunt.

Celinda and Deryn stayed with Trinna for a while.

As far as the guards were concerned, everybody had attacked the Prince in self-defence. He was a hulking beast of a man who threatened everybody, and genuinely, unapologetically, wanted to kill people for the most asinine of reasons. He was a bad, bad man, and though they obviously did not endorse killing, they endorsed protecting oneself. From what they could see, and from what they gathered during questioning, all the actions of the day were justified.

They appointed a new Chief of the Guard later in the week, and hardly mourned the loss of Leonard Garden-Hand. He had, after all, pushed a girl out of a window. There are many things that can be forgiven, but pushing people out of windows is never, ever one of them. That is fundamentally irredeemable.

Paloma reunited with her mother. The rest of the Council reunited with their friend.

Two ex-guards made a life together in a port town overseas.

A former executioner wandered for a while, unsure of what made him who he was.

The city moved on.

The world moved on.

Together, the people moved on.

They moved on together, as Robins in the Day.

# Epilogue One: The Corridor, by David Barry

You were in a corridor. It was dark, only vaguely and dimly lit from an unidentifiable source, and it was full of cobwebs. It seemed to be at its widest near the entrance, narrowing as you walked towards the end. If there was in fact an end. There was no way of knowing, as the cobwebs seemed to be repeating themselves, giving the feeling of walking in circles even though you were walking in a straight line.

There also seemed to be a gradual decline. It was so subtle, so smooth, that you wouldn't notice it unless you were really paying attention, which, after a while, you weren't. At first you wondered where you were going, how deep and how far this corridor with its gradually closer and closer walls could possibly go, where it could lead and what you would find, but after a few thousand steps you just really didn't care. You were walking for the sake of walking, and all the arms in the world couldn't hold you back. Not that they stood a chance anyway. They'd tried to hold you back before you walked down here. Those arms attached to those humans, all of them telling you to live the same life day in and day out. You decided to ignore them and walk down the corridor. You weren't sure if you regretted it. You weren't sure if regret mattered any more. You weren't sure it ever had mattered.

Was it getting lighter, or had your eyes adjusted to the darkness? Were the cobwebs thinning? Was the hard concrete floor replaced by a soft carpet that appeared to be bright red? Yes. All of those things were happening. It brought you back into reality just in time for you to realise you were about to walk into a door. The walls were close now. They were lightly grazing the hairs of your arms, which stood on end in either cold or anticipation. Or both. The door seemed rather disappointingly plain. Wood. Polished. Round handle.

You knew where this corridor was.

You knew how to get in.

You knew what was on the other side of this door.

You'd never seen it, but you knew. It was everything you'd ever wanted and nothing you'd ever had. You were part of the ones who walked the corridor.

The ones who saw what life was and didn't want anything to do with it. The ones who saw the wolves in their formal clothes with the glint in their eye telling you to buy their products which will make you addicted to other products. The ones who saw the world as the hunting ground it really was, the lion's pride with the people at the top of the food chain lording it over everybody else.

You were one of Them. You left. You went missing. And you walked away. Down the corridor. Thousands of steps on hard concrete. Did your feet hurt? Did you fall? Did you regret coming down here?

Did you open the door?

## Epilogue Two: The Backwards Pack, by Marian Stoke-Hood

"Heaven help him!" said William's father feelingly.

William's father stumbled as his crutch slipped. It didn't hurt, but what little breath he had was knocked out of him. He hobbled and scraped back to the house, having seen enough. There is only so much time in a day and devoting too much of it to watching your only child ride recklessly into the sunset can really eat into valuable hours allotted for sitting and breathing easily.

He didn't know what on Earth William hoped to accomplish. He was being stupid, as usual. He heard people in the tavern talking about a werewolf, in the cave at the foot of the mountains. Nobody's ever even seen a werewolf but yet off William rides to slay the rumoured beast. Absurd. Absolutely ridiculous. Heaven help him.

There was stew cooking on the fire. It smelled as though it was going to be basically edible and the colours it wore as it bubbled away heavily implied that the flavour was going to be entirely unremarkable but not exactly unpleasant. Outside, the galloping of hooves had been replaced with the general mess of rain. Rain had always seemed to William's father like a lazy child throwing all of its toys on the floor without bothering to put them away, not thinking of the consequences of its actions. William's father knew many children who didn't think of the consequences of their actions. William's father knew them personally and closely. William's father was William's father. Heaven help him.

However, he had to admit that the sound of rain combined with the warm, deep effervescing of the stew were very relaxing. In his armchair with his crutch set aside, he could almost fall asleep. But only almost. He could definitely very nearly fall asleep. But he had no intention of getting to that point. He wouldn't fall asleep, but it was possible that he could. He shouldn't.

William's father woke up to the sun piercing through his window. The stew wasn't bubbling. The stew wasn't even there. Confused, he stood, leaning against his crutch and investigating the empty pot, thinking somebody had broken in, but he could see no broken windows. But then he heard something.

Something made a sound. Something was upstairs, at the end of the hall, on the left. William's room.

"William?" asked William's father, rising in intonation towards the end of the word, perhaps a little more than he meant.

More noises. Steps. Hurried. Down the corridor, down the stairs. William! It was William after all.

"Well thank heavens you're back, boy. Knew you wouldn't find anything. You'd come back here and throw the werewolf's fur over the carpet, you said. You'd mount his head above the fireplace."

William said nothing. He just cocked his head slightly to the side.

"Don't look at me like that, my lad. I mean no ill spirit, I'm glad you're home unscathed, in one piece! I hope nothing bit you, we can't afford the healer's price for fixing an infection."

William said nothing. He just inhaled deeply.

"So what happened? Hang on, let me sit down."

William's father sat back in his chair, and set his crutch down next to it, then gestured for William to regale the gloriously anticlimactic tale.

"What was in the cave then? A couple of rats? A bear?"

William said nothing. He just looked over to the fireplace.

"What are you looking for? You ate all of the stew! That's a lot of stew for a lad your size, you must've been hungry. A bear, then?"

William finally spoke, eyes wide but looking at nothing in particular.

"I was hungry." he said.

Silence fell into the room and found an awkwardly tense situation, like walking in on somebody else's argument with their spouse.

"I was hungry. I ate the stew. It was fine. But I was hungry. So I ate the horse. It was good. But I'm hungry." he continued.

"It wasn't a normal werewolf, father. It was a wolf... Just a wolf. But then the moon came. The moon came out and shone down on the wolf. And it was a man, and I was a man too."

William's father's brow shifted. His hand curled around the handle of his crutch. Rays of sun pierced through the window arrogantly as though they thought they owned the place. They didn't. The sun doesn't own anywhere, it just makes things hot, but this moment was heated enough without the need of a star of any size. Lights in the sky were unnecessary and inconveniently placed. The sudden glint in William's eye was enough to light up the entire situation.

"I'm hungry, father."

His voice was rough like the bristles of a werewolf's fur, though nobody has ever seen a werewolf. If somebody theoretically sought one out and didn't think of the consequences of their actions, their fate would be in heaven's hands. William's father knew many children who didn't think of the consequences of their actions. William's father knew them personally and closely. William's father was William's father.

Heaven help him.

## Epilogue Three: The Painted Mermaid, by Areneld Vastonia

The world is vast, and covered in water. Water is sucked from the oceans by the heat of the sun and then water falls on the mountains, forming rivers, returning to the ocean. There are great still lakes, cascading waterfalls, and of course the occasional puddle.

With all this water it comes as no surprise that there are strange and wonderful things that have evolved to live in it. Schools of fish clinging to currents, mighty and powerful mammals batting their tails just above the surface, and bizarre plant life that survives in conditions no land plants could ever tolerate.

But even more wonderful than all of this are the Dwellers.

It is said that thousands of years ago, an orphaned princess walked the shores of a distant land. As she walked, she prayed to the gods of the water to bring her parents back, looking skyward, tears in her eyes, until she looked down and realised she had walked over the water, far from the beach. Her footprints were barely visible away on the sand, but stood there easily visible were her parents. Her prayers had been answered, her family was alive and well, but she could not reach the shore again no matter how quickly or determinedly she ran. They seemed to get further and further away until they were mere dots on the horizon, and the princess accepted her fate.

She stood still now, and slowly sank into the ocean until it swallowed her whole; for the gods work in peculiar ways. Their whims, the people say, are as unpredictable as the tides.

But then, months, or perhaps years later, a young fisherman sailed out to deep waters, intending to catch dinner for his family for the rest of the month. As he cast his net into the water however, it ensnared something unexpected and unknown. Caught within his net was a curious creature, the upper half of a human but the lower half of a fish. It had gills, flowing hair and wore only the torn remnants of a gown once beautiful. He pulled the creature back into his boat, tearing open the net to claim his prize, and under the light of the early sun, her form began to change. Her lower half entered a metamorphosis, becoming human legs once more. The fisherman thought perhaps he was so drunk he'd forgotten about the actual drinking part. The creature kept her gills through the transformation, and she opened her eyes to reveal that they were completely black, smiling at the boy.

From here, the legends vary. Some say the fisher boy and the creature were swept away by a sudden tidal wave, some say the creature caught the boy in his own net and dragged him away to sea, others say that the creature asked the boy three questions and then allowed him passage into her underwater palace.

The legend remains consistent on one point, however. The creature was the old orphaned princess, having been consumed by the sea as payment for the resurrection of her parents, and she stole the boy away to become like her too.

And these two, the orphaned princess turned Salt Water Queen, and the young fisherman turned Boy King of Waves, were the first of the Dwellers. The Dwellers have the same power of transformation as the Salt Water Queen. On land or on deck, they grow human legs, but in the water, they become elegant hybrids of human and fish, effortlessly moving through the water. They feed on fish and seaweed primarily, but it is said that they enjoy the beverages carried by pirate boats and occasionally enjoy the pirates themselves. They can be found in the deepest of oceans, only seen in shallow waters occasionally when they decide to raid the ports of patriarchal cities.

It is unknown if the Salt Water Queen or the Boy King of Waves still live, but their lineage lives on through the Nighteyes, the royal family of Dwellers. Their eyes, unlike all other Dwellers, are as black as the darkest night, as deep as the ocean floor, and are the only lasting proof of the life of the orphaned princess and the young fisherman, for everything else about their history has been long swept away, mere shreds of a once beautiful dress floating aimlessly on the surface of a faraway ocean.

Or perhaps it lingers still, stuck somewhere, trapped in a numinous bubble between seconds.

# Epilogue Four: Pond Weed: What's it All About?

I've taken you through the life cycle of pond weed. I've taken you through certain attributes of pond weed. I've taken you through everything there is to know about pond weed- everything you ever wanted to know and everything you never knew there was to know. But in seventeen chapters, I still haven't answered your main question, have I? Just what, precisely, is pond weed all about?

My readers, my friends, my beautiful saviours, my frogs hopping on lily pads in the pond of life, my, at this point, family… I have no answer.

The main thing I have discovered about pond weed through all of my research is that pond weed is fundamentally unable to be described. I'm sorry to have taken you through such a long book about pond weed just to hit you with that reveal, but that's just how it's got to be, I'm afraid.

I am literally afraid, though. When I say I'm afraid, I mean it. I'm scared, readers. I'm scared that nobody can describe pond weed. I'm scared that I look at pond weed and feel compelled to write an entire book about it. I'm scared that I can't stop thinking about pond weed.

Do you know anything about pond weed, reader? Do you actually know anything? Did you read this book? I don't think you did. I think you skipped to the end, to the very last page, to see your question answered. Well, bully for you, because there's no answer! There's no answer in this book! You'll never know what pond weed is about, anybody who read the book in its entirety will ever know what pond weed is about, and I will NEVER KNOW WHAT POND WEED IS ABOUT!

I am sorry. I am so very, very sorry.

## Epilogue Five: Poems about Dresses, by Marian Stoke

~Dresses One~

A volunteer.

For sale: Ugly dress.
Brown, tacky, unfashionable.
Used.

An audition.

For sale: Ugly bag.
Fuchsia, leather, uncomfortable.
Used.

A call back.

For sale: Ugly shoes.
Fuchsia, dusty, unnecessary.
Used.

A rehearsal.

For sale: Ugly wig.
Brown, itchy, untamed.
Used.

A show.

For sale. Ugly boy.
Black, awkward, unfashionable, uncomfortable, unnecessary, untamed.
Never used.

Best offer accepted.

~Dresses Two~

The girl in yellow chose the girl in grey.
Their fingers entwined, crossing streams
Winding down the mountain
In a temporary embrace.

They danced together.
Her stream was sure of itself, confident, saccharine
Crashing against the land
Wearing down her surface.

The weather changed.
Her stream was inexperienced, cowardly, stubborn
But moving surely to the ocean
And closer to her face.

They kissed.
Her river of fire burned under cold skin
Harvesting her mountain's forests
As wood for her furnace.

And then she was gone.
The patterns formed by their streams,
Hers of water,
And of frigid monochrome,
And hers of flame,
And of passionate gold,
Lingered as marks on her being.

She looked for her again, for a while.

And then she saw her.
Their streams having wound different paths,
Having spent many summers
Sculpting different rivers,
Fire and water met again,
But never quite boiled,
She had left no marks on her being.

She was forced to accept it.

When the girl in the yellow dress chose the girl in the grey suit,
When their fingers entwined and crossed streams,
When they were winding down the mountain,
And winding around each other,
In their land of burning rivers,
And their world of icy forests,
It was nothing more
Than a temporary embrace.

## ~Dresses Three~

No.

There's no way I'm doing this.
I'm not writing about those dresses.
I'm not writing about the white dress from the first night.
I'm not talking about the blue one from the second.
I'm never, ever talking about the dresses.

I remember every detail, and I wish I didn't.
I remember it hurting.
I remember exactly how the couch felt under me.
I remember exactly how she felt on top of me.

She had this wardrobe full of them, you see.
They were organised by colour, it was sort of cute.
Like a rainbow, almost, except she was definitely missing some colours.
We went shopping together to fill up her wardrobe.
I'm never talking about her dresses.

I remember the first time, and all subsequent times.
I remember what she said and what she did.
I remember what I was wearing.
I remember what she was wearing.

They were her prized possession, the dresses.
In a way I could never live up to them.
But that isn't to say I didn't try.
Hers, to play with, to mess around with.
I'm not talking about her dresses.

I remember saying no.
I remember saying not tonight.
I remember her saying yes.
I remember her saying tonight.

She'd be choosing a dress from her collection.
It always took her a while, of course.
Because of how many she had.

I had to go with whatever choice she made.
I wish I was talking about her dresses.

I'm not talking about the dresses.
You can't make me.
I don't want to think about every time she wore a dress.
I don't want to go back there.
I don't want to remember.

Not tonight.

~Dresses Four~

The first dress was for a show, of course
But the real show
Was pretending she didn't enjoy it

~Dresses Five~

Her dress
Was beautiful
It wasn't like the other dresses

She had
A collection
Of pictures of her in the dress

She didn't
Wear dresses
That often but that was okay

They loved
Each other
Whether they wore dresses or not

Dresses didn't matter any more
They were just dresses
With no connotations

## Afterword

It's quiet, save for voices and doors downstairs. She can hear herself think, at least. Her thoughts can be in order, and she can be calm.

The window won't open very far, which is fine, and there's a fly stuck to the side in a cobweb, which is not. It is also dead, or so she assumes, taking an educated guess. Either way, flies are named for their main skill and ambition, so even if the fly still clings on to life as dearly as it clings to the cobweb, its dreams are undoubtedly beyond revival.

She has spent too long thinking about flies and afterlives and is now quite uncomfortable. She has a lie down. The bed itself is pleasant, if garishly adorned, and helps rebalance the mood of the room, but from here all she can see is a distant view of the unfamiliar section of sky beyond the window which is made ever more unreachable by the emptiness of the walls.

The walls are a faded pink and don't even have any pictures. She wonders what the point of a wall is if it's not even covered in pictures and if it isn't mercifully at least partially green.

Still lying in bed, above the covers, she overhears a conversation in the corridor. People are going out. Shopping, maybe. Hunting, maybe. Stealing, probably. She is happier here, with less noise. Outside her room, sensory overload would be not only vaguely likely but confidently and accurately forecast by her internal meteorologist.

She has to look up meteorologist in a dictionary to ensure she's thinking of the right word. Afterwards, reassured, she turns and rotates the book over and over in one hand, becoming familiar with the shape and size, running her thumb over the ridge of every page. She opens and closes it again and again, trying but not succeeding in distracting herself from nagging thoughts of fly mortality.

She needs a glass of water now. Thankfully there is a jug here, having been laid out for her in the morning, and she doesn't have to go down to the kitchen. She doesn't trust the tap in her room partly because she hasn't got to know it yet but mostly because of the notice in the corner of the mirror explicitly telling her, commanding her in no uncertain terms to definitely not attempt to drink from the tap under any circumstances. In a way it is comforting to know that she can't even if the idea suddenly begins to appeal to her, but she misses the simplicity of the taps at home.

Finishing her water at her temporary desk, she thinks of her real desk at home, and her friends, and her family, and her best friend, and her lover, none of which are too far away all things considered, but between annoyingly pink walls, untrustworthy taps and the looming concept of death as represented by a fly, she rather misses home already.

She stands, looking out over the world and trying to work out exact distances between here and home.

She opens the window and flicks out the fly corpse.

She is Marian, and she is in a bedroom in Celinda's house. The sky, as seen from a different angle than usual, fills with clouds, and Marian's perspective changes. It is one month later.

She begins to realise something.

She begins to realise she is alone.

She begins to realise she has not been to the graveyard in a month.

She begins to realise Jemima is dead.

She begins to realise the bubble she has been forced into is bursting.

She has flicked the fly corpse.

Her life shifts to the past tense.

She stormed down the stairs in Celinda's house and demanded she be able to leave. There was an argument, of course, but in the end, Marian left Celinda's house anyway.

As soon as she stepped outside, and rain fell on her hair, she began to feel sick. But she walked.

As she walked to the graveyard, a snail overtook her. She could barely take more than a few steps a minute. People passed her, moving past and leaving behind. Living. Continuing to exist. Surviving.

And yet still she walked.

There was nothing that would stop her walking. Not the rain, not the snails, not the people, nothing. Not the uneven cobble underfoot pressing hard against the soles of her feet, not the leaves falling from the trees to briefly obscure her vision, not her left wrist sporting a distinct lack of any hint that there was once a hand at the end of it. She would walk on, and she would reach her destination.

No matter what anybody said, or what anybody did, she would get to the graveyard today. She had rested enough.

"One month is too soon." Quilla.

"You need to rest." Xiang.

"Please don't put yourself through this." Paloma.

"I think you need more time." Aleta.

"It won't do you any good." Celinda.

Silence and a disapproving shake of the head. Deryn.

Silence, but no movement. Jemima.

More than the loss of her hand, and more than the city's loss of a sheriff, it had been difficult for anyone to come to terms with the loss of Jemima Hood.

She reached the graveyard, eventually, and approached a grave near the back, under a tall, proud, oak tree. A snail trickled by on top of the gravestone.

"Jemima Hood", the headstone read, "Taken down in her prime".

Marian began to cry.

A hand rested on her shoulder, and she jumped awake.

She was in her home, her house on the road between the docks and the edge of town, in her bed made primarily of pillows, in the arms of the woman she loved.

Jemima Hood was very much a live, as was Marian Hood. They were in bed, together, as was usual.

"You were making noises," Jemima whispered, "Did you have nightmares again?"

Marian nodded, and nestled her head into Jemima's shoulder.

"The usual one," Marian muttered, "Where I lost my hand and you lost… Everything."

"Love," Jemima said, "It's okay. I'll be here until you stop having the nightmares and I'll be here after that. I'll always be here."

"They feel so real," Marian said through almost-sobs, "They feel so incredibly real. I sometimes think I dreamt it all. I think I dreamt the grave, and the green coats, and the daggers, and the axe, and the crown and the sword… I sometimes think it was all made up, in my head."

Jemima kissed Marian's forehead softly.

"All of it was real, love."

"I know. I wake up to you every morning, and that's how I know it was real. I'm just… Glad that when you fell… You landed… Safely."

Jemima squeezed Marian's hand reassuringly.

"Marian Hood. When I'm flying with you, I always land safely."

Thank you for reading.

The story of Marian will continue in the sequel,

Robins in the Shade.

Fly safe.

Made in the USA
Lexington, KY
05 July 2015